WHEN WILLOWS WEEP

WHEN WILLOWS WEEP

G. Sherman H. Morrison

NEW DEGREE PRESS
COPYRIGHT © 2021 G. SHERMAN H. MORRISON
All rights reserved.

WHEN WILLOWS WEEP

ISBN
978-1-63730-440-2   *Paperback*
978-1-63730-537-9   *Kindle Ebook*
978-1-63730-538-6   *Digital Ebook*

The scripture quotations contained herein are from the New Revised Standard Version Bible, copyright © 1989, Division of Christian Education of the National Council of Churches of Christ in the U.S.A. Used by permission. All rights reserved.

For Willow

*Your strength of character,
flexibility in the face of uncertainty,
and compassionate caring for others
are all reflected in these pages.*

To the Monadnock Waldorf School

*For its forty-four years of nurturing students
to contribute fully to their world with courage,
compassion, creativity, and conviction. MWS truly
embodied Rudolf Steiner's vision for Waldorf education:
"Receive the children in reverence, educate them
in love, and send them forth in freedom."*

CONTENTS

	A NOTE FROM THE AUTHOR	9
CHAPTER 1	THE AWAKENER ARRIVES	13
CHAPTER 2	SEEING THE LIGHT	21
CHAPTER 3	HELL ON EARTH	31
CHAPTER 4	BIRDS AND BEES	41
CHAPTER 5	CHOOSE YOUR WEAPON	49
CHAPTER 6	THE FAERY FOREST	59
CHAPTER 7	APRIL FOOLS' DAY	71
CHAPTER 8	A MOONLIT CEMETERY	81
CHAPTER 9	TREES AND TRAINING	91
CHAPTER 10	A FOREST QUEST	105
CHAPTER 11	THE MEDIEVAL CEREMONY	117
CHAPTER 12	MAY DAY ATTACK	127
CHAPTER 13	TYLER'S DARK DESCENT	139
CHAPTER 14	GEHENNA'S LAST STAND	149
CHAPTER 15	THE DAY AFTER	161
	ACKNOWLEDGMENTS	165
	BIBLIOGRAPHY	173

A NOTE FROM THE AUTHOR

What if you discovered there is more to reality? What if there is a whole other layer hidden just below the surface or veiled from the perception of most? And what if not all of it is good? What if you discovered you had special abilities and were expected to use them to protect and save the community in which you live?

I think people who love fantasy stories have a deep sense of longing for there to be more to reality than what they experience on a day-to-day basis. I know this was certainly true for me as an adolescent. It's why I loved J. R. R. Tolkien's *The Hobbit* and *The Chronicles of Narnia* by C. S. Lewis. It's also why I loved immersing myself in the fantasy role-playing game Dungeons and Dragons for many years. All of these provided a way to experience a world in which there was so much more than my own reality offered. There were monsters and magic and epic battles between good and evil. I think this longing for more is especially strong in adolescence, but I also think it never really goes away. I still feel strong echoes of it even as an adult.

I realize now how a big part of what appealed to me about *The Hobbit* and *The Chronicles of Narnia* is something people call "the unlikely hero." Bilbo Baggins, a simple hobbit, ends up being a hero in the grandest adventure of a lifetime. In *The Chronicles of Narnia*, a group of children end up being heroes throughout the story in the magical realm of Narnia.

The idea for this story popped into my head in 2016 when my daughter, Willow, was in the sixth grade of a Waldorf school. During her sixth-grade school year, they made wooden swords in woodworking class, learned a sword dance for the school-wide May Day celebration, and later in the spring even had a Medieval Ceremony in which each sixth-grade student was knighted. It was a magical year, and it made me start thinking about the story you are about to read.

I did not create an entire new world for this story. I was more intrigued by the idea of layering in fantasy elements to the real world. A piece of advice often given to aspiring writers is to "write what you know." I decided to set this story in the town where I live and make my own daughter the protagonist of the story, including the Waldorf school she was attending. True to my love of fantasy, there is magic, there are monsters, and there is an epic battle between good and evil. Also true to my love of the "unlikely hero" theme, a twelve-year-old girl finds herself at the epicenter of the battle.

What I'm aiming for is a contemporary fantasy to which I hope readers can easily and readily relate because of how close it is to the real world. As fantasy writer Lloyd Alexander put it, "Fantasy is hardly an escape from reality. It's a way of understanding it" (A Visit with Lloyd Alexander, 2018). The intersections I wanted to explore in this story include compassion and combat, faith and fantasy, redemption and rejection, free will and fate, and education and ecology.

If you're scratching your head wondering what a "Waldorf school" is, read on! The story will reveal much about this unique approach to education founded by Rudolf Steiner and based on his philosophy and understanding of child development. While there are many unique practices in Waldorf education, one of its overarching themes is incorporating the arts into all academic disciplines at every grade level. It offers a wholistic, integrated approach developing each child's intellectual, artistic, and practical skills. Myths and legends figure prominently in Waldorf education not as mere subjects to read about, but as learning tools deeply experienced. An active church life also plays an important role in the story, and how these two aspects, school and church, intersect is an important thread throughout the tale.

My desire is for this book to be well-received by any adolescent or young adult who has ever attended a Waldorf school, as well as parents of current and past Waldorf students. I also hope the book is appealing to fans of fantasy who are also people of faith. The reason I want *you* to read this book is to enjoy what I hope you will find to be an entertaining story, but even more importantly to grapple with the questions it raises: What are the boundaries or limits of compassion? Does everyone deserve a chance, or multiple chances, at redemption? Perhaps most importantly of all, how would *you* respond if you found yourself suddenly thrust into the middle of an epic battle between good and evil in the very community in which you live?

1

THE AWAKENER ARRIVES

"I am not a teacher, but an awakener."

~ ROBERT FROST ~

"A twelve-year-old girl is a peculiar and wondrous creature: surprisingly mature one moment (at least relative to most boys of the same age) and irritatingly melodramatic the next," a voice said on the radio.

Willow wasn't really paying attention to the program as she sat at the dining table eating lunch, but she did hear that last bit. *I like the sound of "wondrous." Not so sure about "peculiar." Melodramatic? Sure, sometimes. But they're definitely right about boys.* She often noticed how the boys in her sixth-grade class seemed immature compared to the girls.

Although it was a Saturday in March, she had been thinking about school all morning. She was a little sad her sixth-grade teacher, Mrs. Strusas, was going on maternity leave from Elm City Waldorf School to have her first baby. There was a fluttering in her stomach at the thought of meeting her new teacher today, Mr. Leinad Retsof. In most Waldorf schools, it is a standard practice for teachers to make home visits to meet each student before having them in class for the first time. This gives them unique insights into each child they wouldn't otherwise have.

Willow had rejoined Elm City Waldorf for sixth grade after attending a public elementary school for grades three, four, and five when money was too tight at home for private school. She was happy to be back. *I wonder what Mr. Retsof will be like. I hope I like him.* After all, he would be her teacher for the rest of sixth grade as well as both seventh and eighth grades. In a Waldorf elementary and middle school, a class is supposed to stay with the same teacher from first grade all the way through eighth grade. While this is the preference, it doesn't always work out that way.

Munching the last bites of a grilled cheese sandwich, Willow gazed absentmindedly out the window facing the deteriorating barn and the hayfield beyond. She wondered what it was like back when the barn belonged to the little yellow house she lived in with her mom. She wasn't sure why it didn't belong to their house anymore. Mom had mentioned something about it having been "subdivided" off the property (whatever that meant) decades ago. It didn't bother her it wasn't theirs because it was in bad shape. In the fall when people drove up Old Gilsum Hill Road to pick apples at the orchard at the end of the road, many would stop to take pictures of it. *Why in the world do people want to photograph an old, falling-apart barn?*

Something moving across the hayfield caught her eye: a young man wearing a brown leather jacket and khakis, with a guitar slung over his back. She couldn't help but smile. This *had* to be Mr. Retsof, her new teacher. Only a Waldorf teacher would manage to arrive not by car but on foot, traipsing across a field from a direction that made no sense as the road dead-ends at the apple orchard.

Mom was outside tending flowerbeds that might soon show signs of life if winter was really over. Rarely was this the case in New England on the eve of spring equinox. Mom also noticed the young man coming toward the house. She stood up from her work to meet him. After they exchanged greetings, Mr. Retsof came into the house. Willow was relieved Mom wouldn't embarrass her by trying to join what is supposed to be a one-on-one meeting between teacher and student.

Willow rose so abruptly to greet him that she knocked over the chair she'd been sitting in. It made a terrible racket as it clattered to the hardwood floor. She could feel her face turning red as she quickly righted the chair. She was somewhat surprised Mr. Retsof was only a little taller than her own five feet seven-and-three-quarters inches.

He smiled and extended his hand to her. Waldorf teachers always shake hands when greeting a student, whether in school or out.

"Good afternoon, Willow. It is a pleasure to meet you."

His handshake was firm but gentle. It was sort of comforting, like when she got hugs from relatives she hadn't seen for a long time.

"Good afternoon, Mr. Retsof. Welcome!"

The teacher seemed content to stand in silence and study the scene. *Am I supposed to do something? Say something? Should I offer him a glass of water?*

What came out of her mouth, however, was "You look like Buddy Holly."

Why did I say that? To be fair, his hair and glasses *did* make him resemble the 1950s rock-n-roll star she'd seen when looking through old record albums at her grandmama's house.

He raised his eyebrows as he considered her statement before saying, "He was a great musician, so I will consider that a compliment." Glancing out the kitchen door window he added, "I noticed the lovely willow tree outside."

"My mom and dad planted it the year I was born," Willow said, internally breathing a sigh of relief.

"They picked the perfect spot for it with the little stream right there," Mr. Retsof observed. "Willows do like to have their feet wet."

The image of a willow tree dipping its "feet" in the water made her giggle.

Mr. Retsof was appreciating the exposed hand-hewn beams of the house. "Does your house have a name? It feels like it's been here a long time."

Willow had heard both her parents, but especially her dad, tell the history of this little house so many times over the years. She knew most of it by heart.

She recited what she knew: "We call it The Old Chestnut, not because of the color but because of those big beams. We think they're chestnut, but we're not totally sure. The house was probably built in the 1790s. My dad has traced the deed all the way back to 1812 himself. It goes back further than that, but those records are in some kind of secret vault or something. They don't let just anyone in there."

Mr. Retsof nodded in approval as he removed his guitar and took a seat on the couch in the living room. Willow sat back down in her chair at the dining table, turning it to face him. At the far end of the long living-dining-combination room was an upright piano as well as an antique pump organ.

Her mother's violin hung on the wall above the piano. Willow's own violin lay on the piano bench.

After taking a moment to survey these surroundings, Mr. Retsof asked, "You play the violin?"

"Yes," Willow answered with pride in her voice. "I've been playing violin since I was four. I've also been learning to play my mom's flute. I don't play piano, though. The organ doesn't work. I think it needs new bellows or something."

Mr. Retsof began picking out a somewhat melancholy melody on his guitar. "Does this tune sound familiar to you?"

She did recognize it, though it took her a moment to remember what it was. "Yes! It's a song we sing in church at Christmastime. Lully Lullay or something like that? I really like it, but I don't remember many of the words right now."

"What do you like about it, Willow?"

"Um…I like how it sounds kind of sad, but then right at the end feels more…hopeful?" Willow's favorite hymns were always in a minor key.

"Yes, you're right about how the notes sound. The music is mostly in a minor key, which gives it that sad feeling, but then the last chord changes one note by just a half-step to make it a major chord, which is why it feels more hopeful to you. It's a very old hymn of the church whose words were written back in the 1500s. But long before the church wrote the words of "Coventry Carol" to go with the music, there were other words that went with this tune." He continued playing and softly sang these words:

> *When darkness drear fills all with fear,*
> *Dry not the glist'ning tear,*
> *To catch the Light and shine hope bright,*
> *Only when willows weep.*

Bend, sway, arise before mine eyes,
Thy pow'r, thy strength ne'er dies.
Shine forth the Light and darkness smite,
Bless'd now when willows weep.

Take up thy rod and go abroad,
Fight now you must for God.
Comes now thy time, wisdom sublime,
Flowing when willows weep.

When he finished the song, they sat in silence for what felt like a long time. Willow sensed she somehow belonged to this song, but she didn't know why she had this feeling or what it could mean. *How can a person belong to a song?* A church hymn she knew and loved had older words about willows? It was too random to be random, if that made any sense. It felt both odd and intriguing.

Does he want me to say something? What should I say? She was freezing up, as she sometimes did in situations when put on the spot (although oftentimes those moments were entirely of her own making). "I, uh, didn't know there were, uh, other words to that song."

Mr. Retsof smiled and waved away her anxiety. Changing the topic he asked, "What do you know about your name?"

Willow paused slightly before saying, "Nothing, really. I mean besides, you know, willow trees."

"Then I have a homework assignment for you to complete before you come to school Monday morning. I want you to find out whatever you can about your name. Why your parents gave it to you, and what you think it would mean for you to *live* your name."

"Sure, Mr. Retsof. I can do that." Willow wasn't excited about the idea of homework between now and Monday morning, but the assignment itself sounded pretty interesting.

"Good. I look forward to hearing you share with the class what you find out," he said with a nod of his head.

He stood up and slung the guitar across his back. Willow stood up as well. He extended his hand for a farewell shake. "I think it's going to be a very interesting spring for you, Willow."

She had no idea what to say to that. *Okay…great, I guess?* "See you Monday, Mr. Retsof."

And with that, Mr. Retsof walked outside, said goodbye to her mom, and set off back across the hayfield.

This whole encounter wasn't at all what she expected, but she also hadn't known what to expect. It didn't last nearly as long as she thought it would. He seemed to know a lot about music. He could sing and play guitar at the same time. And he really did look like Buddy Holly. There was also something a little mysterious about him. The music and words of the song lingered in her mind.

Her mom would want her to say something about this visit, so she walked outside. The sunlight brought out the red in her hair to a striking degree. She stood still with her hazel eyes closed, enjoying the warm sunshine on her face. *Could spring really be here already? That would be so nice.*

"Well?" her mom asked. "What do you think of this new teacher?"

"I think…" Willow paused for dramatic effect before saying, "…he's *awesome*. I think he's gonna to be the best teacher *ever*!"

Later that night Willow drifted off to sleep feeling good about her new teacher and excited to research her name. Several hours later, however, at precisely half-past midnight when the spring equinox arrived, a nightmare interrupted her otherwise peaceful sleep:

Willow dared not take another step back or she would surely burst into flames from the raging inferno engulfing the barn behind her.

There was nowhere to run. The field before her was alive, writhing with... What were they? Hundreds of feral dogs? But they were more than that. There was something undeniably evil about them.

They circled round and round in a whirling mass, growling and snarling and barking, baring their yellow fangs. Their glowing-red eyes were always on her throat. Willow put a hand to her neck.

One of the creatures separated from the rest and slowly approached her. It never took its eyes from her. It was nearly twice the size of all the others: the leader of the pack. Its scraggly fur was a jumble of jagged black and gray stripes.

Its piercing gaze bore into Willow's very soul as if to say, "I smell your fear."

It sprang at her, jaws gaping wide. Willow could clearly see double rows of razor-sharp teeth...

Gasping for breath, Willow bolted upright in her bed. Drenched in sweat, heart pounding, both hands protecting her neck, it took a few moments for her to realize the evil dog attack was just a bad dream: a very bad dream indeed.

2

SEEING THE LIGHT

―

"Light thinks it travels faster than anything but it is wrong. No matter how fast light travels, it finds the darkness has always got there first and is waiting for it."

~ TERRY PRATCHETT, *REAPER MAN* ~

Willow was about to shovel a big spoonful of cereal into her mouth when she noticed her mom was glowing: not figuratively, but literally *glowing*. Some kind of light was emanating from the middle of her chest. Willow rubbed her eyes, thinking she must not have slept well because of the nightmare. Nope, Mom was still glowing. It was a warm, comforting kind of light, pure white but not blinding. And then it faded. *What in the world was that?*

Her mom was standing at the kitchen sink washing dishes. "Willow, is something wrong?"

Giving herself a little shake, she replied, "No, I was just…thinking about a bad dream I had last night. I was being attacked by wild dogs out in the hayfield." She thought she'd better leave out the part about them being *evil*. Mom would probably freak out if she said anything about that.

Wiping her hands on a towel as she finished the dishes, Willow's mom said, "Oh, by the way, look what I found going through a stack of your drawings and things when I was cleaning out the closet in the family room."

She pulled a piece of paper out from a pile on top of the fridge and handed it to Willow. On one side Willow had drawn a picture in crayon of a tree and several different faeries. There was a green tree faery, a blue water faery, and a pink flower faery. On the other side she had written a note to the faeries:

Dear Faeries,

I have some questions that I would like to ask.

Question #1: Why is it the rule that you cant show yourselfs?

Question #2: can you make a people fly?

Question #3: If you are not aloud to show yourself then can you at least write notes to me and I write back?

Oh! I am sorry for the mistakes, I need more practice.

Her mom went on, "This is so cute. You were really into faeries when you did this, probably when you were five or six. I love how sincere you were about it."

Looking at the drawing and the note, Willow felt echoes of the deep longing she had back then of wanting to see faeries. At that age she believed in them but couldn't understand why they stayed hidden. Somewhere deep inside she still wanted them to be real, though she was long past the age for such things.

It was Sunday morning, which meant going to church. Her father was going to be singing an anthem, which was always a treat for her. She and her parents loved music and performing on stage in theatrical productions of all kinds. She especially liked being in shows with her parents, though it was unlikely all three of them would ever share the stage again after the divorce. A twinge of sadness tried to make itself felt within her, but she quickly squashed it. She didn't understand the *why* of their divorce, but she was relieved they were on good terms. She always slept at the little yellow house on Old Gilsum Hill Road, but she saw her dad every day. In fact, after church she planned to hang out at her dad's apartment and do the homework assignment Mr. Retsof had given her yesterday.

When she and Mom made the ten-minute drive downtown and the tall, white steeple came into view, Willow smiled. She enjoyed going to church because she liked singing hymns. The sermons were sometimes interesting. The snacks at coffee hour afterwards, however, were *always* worth it.

She also liked how everyone knew the building as a landmark in Keene, New Hampshire. All she had to say was "the big, white church at the head of Central Square" and everyone knew what she was talking about. Every time she saw the steeple, she thought about what she learned in third-grade history class, which focused on local history. During the Great Hurricane of 1938, the fierce winds snapped the steeple off and sent it stabbing down through the roof of the sanctuary.

These thoughts were quickly replaced by what she anticipated most about today's service, which was hearing the new senior minister preach for the first time. When the previous minister left and the church needed to find a new minister, it seemed to take forever. After nearly eighteen months, it was the Reverend Gayle B. Hyacinth who was finally called to serve. She would be the first female senior minister of the United Church of Christ in Keene since its founding in 1738. When Willow finally understood how big a deal this was, she was as excited as everyone else was about it.

Sitting beside mom in their usual box-like pew, it dawned on her she'd been coming to this church her whole life. Everything felt deeply familiar to her in a comforting kind of way. It was only when other people pointed things out that she realized how different it was from other churches.

The sanctuary was on the second floor, which she learned was traditional for New England congregational churches. There were tons of windows, but none were stained glass. This would have been considered too extravagant for the church's thrifty members of yesteryear. Most everything was painted white. The only other colors were the dark-red carpeting, the caramel-colored seat cushions in the pews, and the dark-stained wood of the pulpit. She loved looking at all the carved woodwork details of the columns that held up the balcony spanning the rear and sides of the sanctuary: skilled craftsmanship performed by true masters centuries ago.

Then the sound of the huge pipe organ and her father's singing filled the sanctuary from the choir loft behind her. Glancing up over her shoulder, Dad winked at her as his baritone voice belted out a soaring anthem. The words were based on excerpts from the opening verses of Psalm twenty-seven:

The Lord is my light and my salvation;
whom shall I fear?
The Lord is the stronghold of my life;
of whom shall I be afraid?

When evildoers assail me
to devour my flesh—
my adversaries and foes—
they shall stumble and fall.

Though an army encamp against me
my heart shall not fear;
though war rise up against me,
yet I will be confident.

For he will hide me in his shelter
in the day of trouble;
he will conceal me under the cover of his tent;
he will set me high on a rock.

As the anthem ended, Pastor Gayle stood in the pulpit in a white robe and looked out at her new congregation. *How old is she?* Willow wondered. She was terrible at judging the age of anyone older than her parents. Something grandmotherly about the new minister made Willow guess maybe in her sixties. Her blonde hair was shorter than shoulder-length. She was plump in a pleasant sort of way. Her black-rimmed glasses gave her an air of intelligence and wisdom as she began to preach.

"Choosing a topic for a first sermon as a newly-settled senior minister is a daunting task, so I've decided to start at the beginning, and anyone who loves *The Sound of Music* as much as I do will know the beginning is a very good place to start! Listen to these opening words in the Book of Genesis, chapter one, verses one through four:

"'In the beginning when God created the heavens and the earth, the earth was a formless void and darkness covered the face of the deep, while a wind from God swept over the face of the waters. Then God said, 'Let there be light,' and there was light. And God saw that the light was good; and God separated the light from the darkness.'

"This is what I want to talk to you about this morning: Light. Those first verses of the Bible are quite clear: Light is good. God didn't say the darkness was good, so we naturally assume darkness must be bad. I think all of us, as humans, understand this distinction between light and darkness deeply and intuitively at the very core of our biological beings. Why? It is for the very simple reason that we can't see in the dark! Most of us, whether we care to admit it or not, are at least a little bit afraid of the dark."

Am I afraid of the dark? I remember being nervous about going to bed when I was little. I don't feel like I'm afraid of the dark now.

"If you found yourself outside in the wilderness on a pitch-black night when clouds obscure even the moon and stars and there are no artificial lights around, can you honestly tell me you wouldn't feel at least a little unnerved if not downright scared? You realize what a disadvantage you're at out in the wilderness when it's dark. Every little sound you hear becomes a potential threat. After all, there are creatures in the night who *can* see in the dark, and they might see you as a rather tasty morsel."

Well, yeah, when you put it that way, who wouldn't be afraid of the dark? I think this new minister could tell a good ghost story if she wanted to.

"Many will say we outgrow being afraid of the dark, but I don't think most of us ever really do. We just rely more on artificial light to chase the darkness away. All we have to do is flip a light switch on and all is well. Light is *good*! In the Bible, people who had direct encounters with God or angels always saw *light*, like the shepherds to whom an angel appeared to announce the birth of Jesus or when Peter was rescued from prison by an angel. Saul on the road to Damascus was blinded for three days by the divine light he saw.

"So yes, light is very important to Christians. We strengthen our faith by reading the Bible because it is God's Word for us and a primary source of enlightenment. As the psalmist said in Psalm 119 verse 105, 'Your word is a lamp to my feet, and a light to my path.'

"We need God's Light because let's face it, we all are still afraid of the dark, afraid of all the death, destruction, calamities, and struggles happening in the world. But even in the face of darkness, we needn't feel afraid. As Gerald sang in the anthem before the sermon, 'The Lord is my light and my salvation; whom shall I fear? The Lord is the stronghold of my life; of whom shall I be afraid?' We all have the Light of Christ in us. We just have to let it shine! And we must always strive to *see* the Light of Christ in others, whether they are believers or not."

Willow recalled the moment earlier during breakfast when she saw a light shining from within her mom. *Is that what she's talking about?* There was a nervous kind of fluttering in her tummy when Pastor Gayle looked directly at Willow and said, "Some of us can see the Light of Christ in people more clearly than others." Willow glanced around to see if it was someone else the pastor was looking at.

Pastor Gayle continued addressing the rest of the congregation, "But take a look around you. Take a look at the person to your left and to your right, in front of you and behind you; your church family right here in this sanctuary."

This was not something most of these rather reserved churchgoers were used to, so the discomfort was palpable as people apprehensively glanced at each other. "Can you see the Light of Christ in them?"

As Willow looked around, sure enough, that same warm, white light was glowing from within each person, just like she had seen in her mom. She nodded at the pastor, who returned a barely noticeable nod of acknowledgment. Being surrounded by glowing people was thrilling and odd and beautiful. She'd never experienced anything like it. *Are other people seeing this? It doesn't seem like it, but Pastor Gayle seems to know I can see it. She must be able to see it too. Makes sense a pastor might be able to see it, but why me?*

A chill washed over her unexpectedly. The hair on the back of her neck stood up. A dull ache of dread formed in the pit of her stomach. Something was behind her. Something dark and heavy. Willow turned her head enough to see a woman standing in the open double-doors that led from the sanctuary to the narthex. The woman was thin, wearing all black garments that looked as if she were attending a funeral of some bygone era. A thick veil entirely obscured her face. What lay beneath that veil?

Willow shuddered as she saw pure darkness emanating from this woman. It was like thick, black smoke, moving around her on the ground as if it were alive. The warm, white light shining in those who were near the woman in black began to dim. Their shoulders slumped. The expressions on their faces became more worried than worshipful. But none of them seemed to physically *see* the woman in black. Willow tried to scream, but nothing came out of her mouth.

She wanted to get up and run away but she couldn't move. She was paralyzed by fear, just like in her nightmare.

Pastor Gayle seemed to be speaking directly to the apparition. "It can be difficult sometimes to see the Light of Christ in others, but it is there." Staring hard at the woman in black, Willow saw no light in her, just a reddish glow like a smoldering ember. A raging anger simmered there, barely contained. Deeper within was yet something else, something bluish, but she couldn't tell what it was.

A seething, screeching voice erupted into her head: "Foolish child. You believe these words? Your sacred scriptures say God created light and called it good. But darkness existed long before that, and darkness will remain long after the light has been *extinguished*."

Willow often talked to herself in her own head, but to have a voice not her own in her head was beyond disturbing. *Is this voice coming from the woman in black? It must be. It sounds like she looks.* It hurt far more than the worst headache she'd ever had. Panic coursed throughout Willow's body, but she couldn't move or tear her gaze from the dark lady. *I feel like my heart is going to explode.*

Pastor Gayle went on despite the dark woman's oppressive presence: "It is up to each of us, as believers in and followers of Jesus, to shine the Light of Christ everywhere we go. The Gospel of Matthew chapter five, verse sixteen says, 'Let your light shine before others, so that they may see your good works and give glory to your Father in heaven.'

"We shine the Light of Christ when we help those in need, when we act with the same kindness and compassion Christ showed the outcasts of society. The Light of Christ is the Light of Love. As the Reverend Dr. Martin Luther King Jr. said, 'Darkness cannot drive out darkness; only light can do that. Hate cannot drive out hate; only love can do that.'"

The voice ripped into Willow's head again. "The darkness is inescapable. Wherever light goes, the darkness is there, waiting to swallow it up."

I feel like I might faint. I hope I don't hit my head when I fall. Mom's gonna freak out.

In her peripheral vision, Willow saw Mom lean toward her and could barely hear her whisper, "Willow, what's going on with you? You look really pale."

Pastor Gayle raised her voice, speaking firmly and clearly: "And the Light of Christ *will* shine on forever. As it says in John chapter one, verse five, '*The light shines in the darkness, and the darkness did not overcome it.*' Amen!"

With that rebuke, the woman in black vanished and Willow crumpled into her mother's lap.

3

HELL ON EARTH

"Hell is empty and all the devils are here."

~ WILLIAM SHAKESPEARE (ARIEL IN *THE TEMPEST*) ~

I've got to speak with the pastor. I'm starving. I really have to pee. These three primary concerns were vying for Willow's attention as the service came to a close.

After the woman in black had vanished, Willow didn't really faint. It felt very safe to have her head in mom's lap and feel her stroking her hair. Willow's sense of terror quickly faded. The service had gone on as if nothing out of the ordinary had occurred. There were prayers, more hymns, collecting the offering, the pastor's benediction, and the organist's triumphant postlude. *Who was the evil woman in black? Did Pastor Gayle really know what was happening?*

As she and her mom made their way down to the dining hall in the basement of the church, she kept one eye on her mom, wondering if she really had been oblivious to what had happened during the service. As if in reply, Mom said, "You seemed distracted during the sermon. Are you okay?"

"I'm fine. I just have to pee and I'm starving." Reaching the dining hall, Willow slipped into the women's restroom. She thought how easily she could have peed her pants when the woman in black made her appearance. She'd never been so scared in all her life, not to mention hearing the dreadful voice in her head. *Why is all of this happening today? And why is it all happening to me? What does it all mean?* She felt sure Pastor Gayle would have some answers, but the rumble in her stomach told her she needed to make another pitstop first—snacks!

The congregation of this church may be generally frugal, but they were *serious* about their coffee hour. Today's spread was typical, including all manner of home-baked treats such as cookies, sweet breads, cupcakes, brownies, and more. Rounding out the offerings were veggie trays with dip, plates of crackers and cheese, and fresh fruit platters. Stacking a rather large amount of food onto a tiny paper plate, Dad suddenly appeared at her side.

"Hey you! What did you think of my solo this morning?"

"It was really good! That one is, like, your power anthem. I don't know how you hold that last note so long!" Willow loved how Dad always sought out her opinion first after any kind of performance.

He smiled, saying, "I was seriously running out of breath but managed to hang on. Two more beats and I probably would have fainted! Glad you thought it went well. So, Mom and I need to get our heads together about a bunch of scheduling stuff for the coming week. You good for ten or twenty minutes while we do that?" Glancing at her pile of food he quickly added, "Like I have to ask. It's going to take you that long to scarf down that pile-o-snacks you have there. Sheesh, kid!" And with that, he was off to find Mom.

After working her way through a good portion of her feast, she realized she must have left her jacket in the sanctuary. She knew she'd better go get it or face Mom's grumpy frown later. With snacks in hand, she made her way up the several flights of stairs from the dining hall to the sanctuary. Her jacket was right where she left it in the pew, so she sat down and continued munching away in the peaceful quiet of the now-empty sanctuary.

On the wall behind the pulpit was the familiar illuminated cross. It was the only overtly religious icon in the whole sanctuary besides the candles. Willow was vaguely aware how some churches displayed the crucifix. The idea struck her as somewhat disturbing. Christ hanging on the cross, wearing a crown of thorns, bleeding and dying. She asked Dad once why some churches had crucifixes and others didn't. He explained it's just a matter of emphasizing different things. "Jesus rose from the dead, so we prefer the empty cross. It's more hopeful that way." She had to agree with that.

She was startled by a voice behind her saying, "Willow! I'm glad you're here."

Willow was relieved it wasn't *inside* her head. She was even more relieved when she realized it was Pastor Gayle.

This was her chance to get some answers, but she had just stuffed the better part of cupcake in her mouth and couldn't say a word. She smiled awkwardly at Pastor Gayle, who saved her from trying to speak.

"Ah, yes, coffee hour snacks! Well, I'm sure you must be wondering about this morning's unseemly hullabaloo, although only you and I were privy to it." Willow nodded her head vigorously while frantically trying to chew and swallow her mouthful of sugary goodness.

"You, my dear, have the God-given gift of Sight, as do I. You can see the Light of Christ in people. You can see if it burns brightly or dimly or not at all. You may also see other creatures most people can't see."

Willow liked the idea of having a gift that made her special, except she didn't like seeing the dark lady. Swallowing the last bit of cupcake, she asked, "Like the woman in black? It was really scary seeing her. Who is she?"

Pastor Gayle paused, as if wanting to choose her words carefully. "All I know is her name—Gehenna—and that she is a powerful, demonic force from Hell."

Willow felt a strong echo of the sense of dread she felt when Gehenna was nearby. "Wait a minute. From Hell? I know the Bible mentions Hell, but my dad says he doesn't believe a loving God would send anyone there for eternal torture. He doesn't think it even really exists."

Pastor Gayle went on, "Oh, Hell is indeed a very real place, but your father is right that our God of love would never condemn anyone to spend eternity there. Going to Hell, when it happens, is a *choice*."

"Who in the world would *choose* to go to Hell?" Willow asked, stupefied by the thought.

"Why indeed. I certainly can't fathom it. But those who do may become powerful enough to do Satan's bidding in this world. Gehenna's power is great indeed to even dare entering a house of worship." The look on Pastor Gayle's face was grave.

"So, you've seen her before?" Willow asked, still trying to get her brain around the idea of any of this being real.

"No, this was my first encounter with her. I was placed in this church because I have dealt with such demons in other places."

Willow let the breath she was holding escape in sigh of relief and said, "Then you'll be able to stop her?" She noticed the slightest furrowing of the minister's brow. Pastor Gayle was worried.

"Oh my, no. This one is far more powerful than any I've ever seen. I would be no match for her."

The knot of fear and dread in the pit of Willow's stomach was making itself known again. "Then who will stop her?"

Pastor Gayle drew herself up straighter and nodded her head in a resolute sort of way. "God has always provided allies in situations like this. There are others in Keene who have divine gifts. I will find them."

Willow wanted to feel reassured by those words, but she didn't feel reassured at all, not one bit. *There's a demon woman from Hell right here in Keene. But why?*

~~~~~~~~~~

Willow was uncharacteristically silent as she and Dad made the short drive from church to his apartment, which was the second floor of a big, Victorian house. He could see her mind was working on something. "Whatcha thinkin' about there, kiddo?"

Dad's question jolted her back to reality. For a second, she considered telling him everything, then realized there was no way she could do that. It was just too much. *What am I thinking about, Dad? You know, just stuff like how I can see the Light of Christ in people, and demons from Hell, which by the way is a real place after all, and how there's a demon lady creeping around Keene. You know, stuff like that.*

Instead she said, "Oh, uh, I've got this homework assignment I have to do before school tomorrow to like, research my name? But the library's not open on Sunday so I guess I have to do it on a computer?"

"Sure," her dad said, "I can set you up on my old laptop."

She rarely sat in front of any computer screen, let alone her dad's old, outdated laptop. Screen time was discouraged at her Waldorf school, a philosophy her parents took far more seriously than those of her peers, to her dismay. All her classmates had cell phones, but not her. She hated missing out on something all her friends had in common.

"What made you and Mom name me Willow?"

Dad looked a little perplexed. "Have I not told you that story? When Mom and I were working up lists of names, we had something like seventy-five different girl names and only a handful of boy names. But we decided to first find out if you were going to be a boy or a girl. After that we just focused on girl names.

"Oddly enough, Willow was not on our list at all! But then two different people at two different times who were visiting us were looking through our baby name books and both mentioned aloud something like, 'Willow. That's a nice name.' And each time Mom and I looked at each other and agreed that it was a nice name.

"So, Willow did end up on our list of names, thought it was rather late in the game. Eventually it came down to you being named Willow or Fiona. We decided if you came out with dark hair we'd go with Willow, and if you came out with red hair we'd go with Fiona. Well, when you were born you had very dark hair, so we went with Willow. Since then your hair has turned out to be red! Honestly, it was just clear your name was supposed to be Willow."

She wondered what it would be like if her name were Fiona instead of Willow. She definitely felt more like a Willow than a Fiona. Maybe that was just from twelve years of being called Willow. Either way, she was happy to be a Willow and wouldn't want any other name.

Her father set up his old laptop on the desk in her room and said, "Okay, I have a web browser open and set to Google, so all you have to do is type in what you want to search and see what you get. If anything goes wrong or you come across something that isn't appropriate, just holler and I'll get it straightened out, okay?"

She gave her dad a very tween eye roll. "Yes, Dad. I think I can handle this without help."

She typed "willow" in the search bar and hit enter. The first item on the results list was the Wikipedia page for Willow, which seemed as good a place to start as any. She read that Willows fall in the genus *Salix*, which includes at least four hundred different species of trees and shrubs found mostly in the temperate and colder regions of the norther hemisphere. The wood from willow trees is strong but also flexible. Willow shoots can be used to make all sorts of woven items such as baskets and wicker furniture. The bark and wood can be made into the kind of charcoal used by artists for drawing and sketching.

She retrieved a pencil and a sheet of paper from her desk and wrote down "strong" and "flexible." She liked the sound of that, though she didn't think of herself as physically strong. She also knew she wasn't very physically flexible, which she felt was the one thing holding her back from being better at ballet. Other dancers seemed to be much more naturally flexible, which drove her crazy.

Going back to the search results page, the next site listed was one with lots of information about willows in culture, literature, religion, and folklore. She saw a story from the

Osage Nation of Native Americans called "Wisdom of the Willow Tree" about a young Native American who sought wisdom from a talking willow tree he called Grandfather Willow. This reminded her of the Disney animated film *Pocahontas* and the wise Grandmother Willow tree who spoke to the Native girl and gave her advice and wise counsel. Willow wrote down "wise" on her sheet of paper. *Am I wise? Maybe, like, most of the time. Probably not all the time.*

She read about how the Buddhist goddess of compassion and mercy, Guanyin, uses a willow branch dipped in pure water to chase away demons. Now that was beginning to sound very practical to her! She jotted down "compassionate" on her paper. Then she saw how willow is one of the four species of plants used in a ritual celebrating the Jewish holiday of Sukkot, symbolizing their devotion to serving God. She wrote down "serves God."

Just as she was about to click the back button to return to the search results page, she got goosebumps all over and something appeared on the screen. It was a small, black orb that grew in size and began to shift in shape and resolve into the dreaded figure of Gehenna, just as she had appeared in church earlier that day, completely hidden underneath her black veil and clothing. In a wave of panic Willow slammed the laptop closed and yelled, *"Dad!"*

Her father quickly appeared in the doorway to her room. "What's up? Everything okay?"

Willow was shaken, but there was the Light in her father. It was strong and comforting enough to calm her down. "Yeah, just wanted to say I'm done with my research, so you can take back your laptop."

"Okay," he said. "Were you able to find what you needed?"

Willow glanced down at her sheet of paper and the words she had written down.

strong

flexible

compassionate

wise

serves God

"I sure hope so. Guess I'll find out soon enough."

Later that night, after Dad drove her back to Mom's house, Willow went to bed not wanting to think about any of this Gehenna business. She finally fell asleep and had another nightmare very similar to the one she dreamt the night before, but slightly different.

Willow was backed up against the burning barn, facing the hayfield full of evil dogs preparing to attack. In her right hand she held a long wooden pole, taller than her. It occurred to her she could use it as a weapon.

The leader of the pack separated from the rest and approached her. This time Willow was ready. She could tell when it was about to pounce. As the beast sprang forward, she swung the pole with every ounce of strength she could muster.

The pole met the snarling head of the hound with a sickening but satisfying crack. The dog's body hit the ground with a thud. Everything was still for a moment.

The beast stirred and quickly rose to its feet. It had only been stunned. It circled back to the swirling mass of its fellow devil dogs where it paused, glaring at Willow.

Then it let loose with a long, piercing, ghoulish howl, like some kind of war cry. As one giant wave, the dogs rushed toward Willow. Her simple, wooden pole would be useless against the onslaught.

Willow awoke abruptly in a state of panic. After the panic subsided, she felt angry. *A stick? Really? A stupid stick was my weapon? Duh.* She settled back down and managed to fall back asleep. All she wanted was for it to be tomorrow so she could have a normal school day with her friends and her new teacher. She was done worrying about demons and having nightmares about devil dogs.

4

BIRDS AND BEES

---

*"Waldorf School Education is not a
pedagogical system but an art—the
art of awakening what is actually
there within the human being."*

~ RUDOLF STEINER ~

I hate being late. Willow's dad was driving away after dropping her off at the front doors of Elm City Waldorf School on Lincoln Street. She had overslept this morning and wasn't quite ready when he came to pick her up. She blamed the nightmares. Reaching for the door handle, she froze as a sudden chill ran down her spine. She sensed she was being watched. Hesitantly, she turned to scan her surroundings.

The houses closest to the school all seemed quiet. Next to the school's small parking lot was a line of trees and bushes, beyond which was a yard where the younger grades had recess. Was there something stirring in the shadows? Quickly entering the school and firmly closing the door behind her, she immediately felt safer and breathed a sigh of relief.

She raced upstairs to the second floor where the middle-grade classrooms were located. If the door to her classroom was closed, she'd have to go back downstairs and report in at the office and be marked as late. The door was still open, and Mr. Retsof was stationed there. Breathlessly, she approached. He extended his hand for the traditional shake and greeting. "Good morning, Willow," he said with a warm smile.

"Good morning, Mr. Retsof," Willow replied while making eye contact, which was an essential part of the greeting, though she didn't know why it was considered so important. This little greeting ritual reminded her of the Waldorf school she attended for second grade when she and her parents lived in Brazil for a year. In Portuguese, the teacher would say "*Bom dia*, Wee-low," to which the expected reply was, "*Bom dia, querido professor*" (Good morning, dear teacher). She liked the Brazilian greeting better because she did dearly love her teacher, even if his pronunciation of her name was a little off. As she entered the classroom, she knew what was coming next.

"Uh-oh, last one in! You're late, *Wee-low!*" It was Tyler. Of all the boys in her class, Tyler was the one who loved to tease the girls. She'd told her classmates one time about how her teacher in Brazil pronounced her name, and Tyler had made it a regular part of his teasing. She didn't mind, though. His teasing was never mean-spirited. His brown hair was always in a state of slight disarray, and he had a nice smile when he wasn't smirking or sneering, which was rare. He was kind of cute, really. *Not that I'd ever admit it in a million, billion years.*

Sitting next to Tyler was Luke, who chimed in, "Technically she's *not* late. The door was still open. It's not about what time you actually arrive, it's about whether the class has started or not."

Willow smiled at him. Leave it to Luke to know the precise "technical" aspects of all rules and policies, or anything else for that matter. He was a walking encyclopedia of facts about everything and wasn't shy about showing off what he knew. Luke's hair was lighter in color than Tyler's, though not quite blond, and he had striking blue eyes as opposed to Tyler's brown eyes.

Ignoring Tyler, Willow plopped her backpack down, sat at her desk, and glanced around the room. Looked like a full house. No one was absent. Four rows of simple wooden desks and chairs in four columns accommodated the sixteen students in her sixth-grade classroom. Willow's desk was on the far-right end of the second row.

Camille, who sat at the desk to her immediate left, leaned over and whispered to her, "Don't you get sick of him calling you *Wee-low*?" Camille was probably Willow's closest friend in the class.

Willow shrugged. "Not really. Could be worse, right?" She could tell Camille clearly wanted to be teased by Tyler with a special nickname of her own.

If there was one thing Willow saw as a big shift in sixth grade compared to earlier grades, it was all the drama that had suddenly sprung up around who has a crush on who. She couldn't help but wonder if all this crushing was going to lead to actual dating. *Yikes! I am so not ready for that.* Not that it hadn't crossed her mind, but the whole idea of it just felt weird to her. She'd been with some of these classmates for most of her life, going all the way back to when they were three-year-olds in the Elm City Waldorf Nursery and Kindergarten. *Being friends is great, but dating? Ugh.*

Her gaze settled on the blackboard extending across the entire front wall of the classroom. The far-right side is always where Waldorf teachers produce their own works of chalk art each week, usually related to something they'd be learning about during Main Lesson. Mr. Retsof had drawn a giant sunflower head in full bloom with two honeybees crawling on its face. The level of detail was stunning and accurate to what she had seen on the sunflowers Mom grew every year around the edges of their garden. She couldn't imagine how long it would take to do a chalk drawing that good.

Mr. Retsof stood at the head of the class with his guitar. "It was a pleasure to meet each of you over the past several days, and I'm excited to begin our educational journey together this week. It seems spring has sprung surprisingly early, which is unusual for this time of year in New England. Let's begin with a song to help keep spring here." He began picking out a simple tune and sang the lyrics of a happy song about winter being over and hearing the robin's song.

Within a few repetitions, they were harmonizing and singing it in rounds. Willow's favorite musical activity, more than playing the violin or flute, was singing. She loved how well her Waldorf class sang together as a group, and today they seemed better than ever. Their voices blended perfectly, and no one was ever out of tune, which wasn't always true for other Waldorf classes. They sang joyfully, including the boys who, in other settings, would be more concerned about "looking cool." And now they had a teacher who was always at the ready to accompany them on his guitar. *This is heaven!*

After singing, Mr. Retsof set his guitar aside. "You all had a homework assignment to complete for today, which was researching your name. Each of you will have a few minutes to tell the class what you found out, and we'll scatter these mini presentations throughout the day. I'll go right down the class list of your first names in alphabetical order." There were a few groans from some who didn't like speaking in front of the whole class, especially when they weren't prepared for it.

A wave of panic washed over Willow. All she had done was jot down a few words that seemed important to her yesterday when she was at her dad's apartment. Gehenna making an appearance on the laptop screen was something she had tried hard not to think about since it happened. She was *not* prepared to make any kind of presentation. She'd be the last one to speak since everyone else's first names started with letters that came before "W." *At least I have some time to think about it.*

Brenden was the first to step in front of the class. He was pretty small for his age, but not the smallest boy in the class. That distinction went to Nate, if only by a little. Brenden's bright-red hair and freckle-filled face was one Willow knew well. He was friendly and fun in an impish sort of way. He was into the circus arts and often rode a unicycle to school. His presentation was short but covered the essentials of how his parents chose his name and that it meant "prince" in Celtic and Gaelic cultures.

Willow wasn't paying close attention when Bridget presented, and Caleb after her, but she perked up when it was Camille's turn. Camille flipped her straight, light-brown hair and noted with a coy smile how her name was of French origins and meant "perfect." Willow smiled at this because it fit her perfectionist personality to a T.

After those four presentations, it was time for Main Lesson. "Our first block together will be on *ecology*, meaning the biology of nature's systems. We're going to focus in on a few interesting themes I think are important to know about. In my drawing on the chalkboard, what do you see?"

Luke's hand shot up instantly as usual. "In the seed head of the sunflower, I see spirals, and if you count the groups of spirals that go together, the number you get is a number in the Fibonacci sequence, where each number is the sum of the previous two numbers in the sequence. If you start with zero, the next number is 0+1=1, then 1+1=2, 1+2=3, 2+3=5, and so on. In your drawing, there are thirty-four clockwise spirals and fifty-five counterclockwise spirals, and those two numbers are in the Fibonacci sequence."

Mr. Retsof seemed startled, though it was the sort of thing Willow and her classmates could count on from Luke: strange but interesting facts. Willow could see the spiral patterns clearly, though she wasn't going to try counting them. Luke had probably done so the moment he arrived at school that morning.

"You're absolutely right, Luke, but we'll save that interesting tidbit for our math block when the time comes. What else do you see?"

Willow decided to chip in at this point with the obvious: "The two bees are gathering pollen they'll use to make honey."

"That's right, Willow," Mr. Retsof acknowledged. "And do you suppose this is the only flower these industrious bees will visit?"

This time Harmonie piped up with a faraway look in her eyes. "I've watched beautiful bees bouncing from flower to flower to flower... Mesmerizing." Harmonie was what Willow would call a little "spacey." Her parents were about as crunchy-granola as they came, and Harmonie had a definite hippie vibe about her.

"Indeed. They will visit many flowers before returning to their hive," Mr. Retsof agreed. "And why might it be important for the bees to visit many flowers on each trip they make to collect pollen?"

By this time, Luke had figured out where this was going and couldn't resist blurting out, "Because visiting multiple plants means spreading pollen around; it's about *pollination!*"

"Correct, Luke. In most plants, the flowers or blossoms need help with pollination. The pollen has to get from the anther to the stigma for pollination to occur so the plant can make seeds to reproduce. Wind and rain can help with pollination, but most of it happens because of bees, flies, moths, butterflies, beetles, and wasps visiting flowers for pollen or nectar. As much as 90 percent of all flowering plants need the help of pollinators, including most of the plants we eat for food or that produce the fruits, vegetables, and nuts we eat."

He then laid out the following instructions: "Start on two pages to go into your Main Lesson Book. Use the top half of one page to make your own diagram of the parts of a flower, labeling all the parts, and on the lower half of that same page, pick one of the pollinators I've mentioned and do a close-up drawing of it and label its main parts as well.

"For the second page, choose your favorite flower and your favorite pollinator and do a full-page color reproduction of the flower being visited by the pollinator. Use any of the books you'll find spread around the classroom about flowers and insects to make your choices. We'll work on these pages both today and tomorrow."

Willow knew instantly what her pairing would be. She loved the sweet-smelling peonies Mom grew in her flower gardens around the house. Their pink, white, and yellow flowers were so large and heavy the plant stems bowed low under their weight. Every few days Mom would cut one or two and float them in bowls of water in the house. They filled any room they were in with the smell of soon-to-come summer. She remembered one day seeing the prettiest little blue butterfly visiting the peonies and the color contrasts were just gorgeous.

Examining the collection of books lining the windowsills on the side of the classroom facing the parking lot outside,

Willow grabbed *Butterflies and Moths of New England*. It was an old book from the look and smell of it. There were lots of detailed color drawings of each species from a variety of angles. *Perfect!* She glanced out the window and gasped at what she saw.

There was a dog sitting in the middle of the parking lot staring up at her. It wasn't just any dog, though. It looked a lot like one of the dogs from her nightmare. It was black and gray, and its eyes were red. The book fell from her hands as Willow rubbed her eyes and looked out the window again. The dog was gone. But she *did* see it, right? And it was one of the demon dogs from her nightmares.

"Hey butterfingers, you dropped this." It was Tyler standing beside her, holding out the book to her. "What's with you? You look like you just saw a ghost or something."

Willow gave him a sarcastic look as she said, "Uh, yeah, cause I see ghosts all the time, Tyler. Don't you?" He smirked at her and went back to his desk.

Willow looked out the window one last time to make sure the devil dog wasn't there and went back to her desk. *Did I really just see what I think I saw? I've had nightmares about those dogs two nights in a row. Maybe it was just a regular dog?*

It took several minutes for her hands to stop trembling enough so she could start drawing.

5

CHOOSE YOUR WEAPON

"The best weapon is the one that will choose you if you're paying attention."

~ ANONYMOUS ~

Spending the rest of Main Lesson working on her drawings was just what Willow needed. She found art relaxing and calming. Searching through the butterflies and moths book, she discovered the little blue butterfly she had seen on the peonies was an Eastern Tailed-Blue. She began her drawings in pencil and then used colored pencils to fill in the brilliant hues as she remembered them.

While the class worked on their Main Lesson pages, more classmates were called on to present their name research. Chloe, the drama queen of the class who always seemed a little too concerned about how she looked to the boys, explained her name meant "young, green shoot." Even Chloe's shoulder-length, wavy, jet-black hair and pale-ivory skin seemed dramatic. She was the one who pushed the edge of the envelope on the school's dress code. Willow admired her cavalier attitude. *Mom would never let me get away with dressing the way she does.*

After Chloe came Emma and Ezra, and then it was Harmonie's turn. In her usual spacey way, she noted her name meant "unity." Her longish light-brown hair had natural blonde highlights and spilled around her shoulders in carefree, untamed curls. She had a knack for harmonizing her own parts when they sang. She played violin like Willow but had a talent for playing fiddle-style, something Willow wished she knew how to do.

When Main Lesson was over, it was off to the basement level of the building for the beginning of a woodworking block taught by Mr. Neilad O'Norscon, a burly man Willow thought looked like a figure out of Norse mythology. He had a thick, white beard and smiling eyes. *He'd make a great Santa Claus.* He also spoke with a slight accent. *Norwegian, maybe?*

The woodworking classroom was one of the largest in the school. The main part had long worktables and stools instead of chairs and desks. There was open shelving along the left wall where works-in-progress were kept, and many cabinets and drawers with woodworking tools and a wide assortment of wood pieces for student projects. The wall behind Mr. O'Norscon's desk was where example project work hung. The right side of the classroom had an opening at the far end leading to another section of the room with a few workbenches and more tool cabinets.

Mr. O'Norscon addressed the class: "The spring woodworking block for sixth grade is when you get to make a handcrafted weapon of wood." The room buzzed with excitement from all the boys in the class.

Typical. Why are boys so obsessed with weapons and fighting?

"A *symbolic* weapon, of course," Mr. O'Norscon emphasized. "The work you do during this block will draw on all the woodworking skills you've developed in previous grades and projects. Successfully making your weapon will require patience and careful attention to detail. You will be graded largely on the precision of your work. And if I catch you horsing around with your weapons, it will have a negative impact on your final grade." This was accompanied by a wave of eye rolling among the boys.

To Willow, mixing sixth-grade boys and weapons seemed like a combination doomed to produce the very behaviors Mr. O'Norscon was warning them against.

He went on: "There are two different weapons you can make during our time together, but you will only have time to make one. You can choose to make a wooden sword, like this one," gesturing to a beautiful wooden short sword hanging on the wall behind him to his right, "or you can choose to make a quarterstaff, like this one," indicating the rather simple-looking wooden pole hanging on the wall behind him to his left. "Choose wisely."

After a short silence, Mr. O'Norscon said, "You may take a few minutes to look at the two different weapons before making your final decision."

The boys instantly jumped up off their stools and crowded around the wooden short sword, admiring it and joking about dueling each other and who would win in hand-to-hand combat. The girls followed the wave of interest in the sword, though they hung back and rolled their eyes at the boys' enthusiasm, feigning disdain.

Willow found herself drawn to the quarterstaff. *Of course everyone's going to choose the sword. Everyone knows you make a sword in sixth grade. Nobody makes a quarterstaff. I didn't even know it was an option.*

Staring at the simple, wooden pole, she remembered her nightmare from last night. *Was "the stick" in my dream supposed to be a quarterstaff? I feel like I'm supposed to choose the quarterstaff, but why? It was totally useless in the dream.*

She was startled from her thoughts by Tyler's voice from across the room. "Hey *Wee-low*, you gonna make a *stick*? You'll be no match for my sword, I can tell you that!"

She turned and opened her mouth to deliver a witty comeback of some sort but didn't have one.

Mr. O'Norscon stepped in to say, "Ah, but here's what you don't know, Tyler. Because of the length of a quarterstaff relative to the sword, the warrior who knows how to use the staff will win against the sword every time, yah? Okay, everybody back to your seats now."

Willow gave Tyler a rather self-righteous smirk as she took her seat. *Am I really going to choose the quarterstaff? I don't want to be the only one. I really like the idea of beating Tyler in a duel though, not that one would ever happen.* Tyler was the most intensely competitive and athletic of all the boys in the class, and it seemed like he was good at every kind of sport. He'd probably be good at combat, too.

Mr. O'Norscon was running down the class list alphabetically by first name. He called out each name, heard their choice, and marked it in his gradebook. Willow was sitting on a stool close enough to his desk she could see him write an "S" next to each name. As she expected, everyone was responding with "Sword."

Willow was beginning to feel less and less sure about choosing the quarterstaff. Mr. O'Norscon called out Tyler's name, he practically shouted, "Sword!" Willow was the only one left. Every classmate had chosen to make the sword.

Willow saw Mr. O'Norscon write a "Q" next to her name. *I still get to make a choice, right? I can still choose the sword. I don't have to be the odd one out.*

Mr. O'Norscon looked up from his gradebook and made eye contact with her. "Willow?"

She wanted to choose the sword, she really did. "Quarterstaff" is what she heard herself say. Everyone was staring at her, and her cheeks were hot.

Mr. O'Norscon stood and said, "For those of you who have chosen to make a sword, you may go to the large red cabinet over there and choose two pieces of wood; one longer piece you'll fashion into the main blade and hilt of your sword, and one smaller piece you'll use to make a guard."

It was immediate chaos as everyone jumped up and raced to select their pieces of wood: everyone except Willow. She sat, dumbfounded at what just happened.

Mr. O'Norscon spoke to her: "Willow, you may come with me to see what I have for you."

She followed him in silence to the far back corner of the workbench section of the classroom where there was a small bulkhead leading to the parking lot outside. Except for its padlocked latch, the narrow closet door to the right of the stairway was a nearly invisible. It was a standard door height, but only about a foot wide.

Mr. O'Norscon retrieved a small key from his pocket and unlocked the padlock. "I've been saving this for a long, long time, Willow." Her heart was racing in anticipation.

Opening the narrow door revealed a large tree branch tucked upright inside the closet. It was as if the closet had been built specifically to house it. "I collected this branch from an ancient Willow tree in the Goose Pond Preserve, not far from where you live. It was the year I became the first woodworking teacher here forty years ago. It is obviously meant for you. After all, in the forty years since this school was started, you're the first sixth-grade student to choose the quarterstaff and not the sword."

Perplexed and honored at the same time, Willow said, "But the branch isn't straight." Indeed, there were many kinks and bends and twists and gnarls.

Mr. O'Norscon nodded. "Aye, but look closer, Willow, to the core of the branch. Tell me what you see."

She stared at the branch and realized what he meant. She visually superimposed a line along the length of the branch. Sure enough, there was a perfectly straight core in the center. She nodded her head in silence.

The woodworking teacher smiled and said, "You see, yah? Your quarterstaff is inside this willow branch. You just have to reveal it."

She took the willow branch from the closet and marched triumphantly back to her seat. She was feeling much better about this choice she wasn't sure she'd even made. It felt more like the choice had been made for her. Now that it was done, however, it felt right to her.

Tyler, of course, couldn't resist calling attention to this. "*Wee-low!* Have fun turning *that* gnarly old thing into a weapon. I still think it won't stand a chance against a sword."

Just you wait, Sir Tyler Tease-a-Lot. As the class was dismissed to go back upstairs, Willow visualized giving Tyler a good smack with her branch. It was very satisfying.

~~~~~~~~~~

Back in their main classroom, there was another round of name research presentations. Juliette, Kara, Lila, and then Luke. Luke got up and provided statistics about how popular his name has been in recent years (of course), and how his name's ancient Greek meaning was "light giving." He also noted that the third Gospel of the New Testament was written by a disciple named Luke, who was a physician. Willow could see Luke becoming a know-it-all doctor, or maybe a world-champion trivia master, if there was such a thing. After Luke, the class heard from Nate and Orion. Then it was Tyler's turn.

In comparison to the many interesting name origins of her other classmates, Tyler's name turned out to be kind of boring. He didn't seem too excited to explain it, either. A lot of family names came from particular occupations, such as Baker, Miller, or Tailor. Although these are usually last names, sometimes they end up as first names. Tyler's name literally meant tile maker or one who works in tiling.

Willow was *loving* this little twist for Tyler, but then it was her turn. *Last one as usual.* By this time, she had memorized the words she had jotted done from her research since she had been repeating them to herself all day.

"Okay, Willow, your turn," Mr. Retsof said. It dawned on her how the assignment she received included "…what you think it would mean for you to live your name." This wasn't something any of her other classmates had talked about. They just mentioned what their name meant and maybe a family story related to their name or their birth.

Am I the only one who got that part of the assignment? Ugh, here we go again. Why is something always "off" for me compared to everyone else? She took a deep breath, went to the front of the class, and paused for a moment to summon up her stage presence skills to appear confident and poised, even though she wasn't feeling that way at all. She blocked out of her mind how everyone was staring at her. She especially blocked out the smirk she knew was on Tyler's face. Then she spoke:

I am Willow

Willow is *strong*

Willow is *flexible*

Willow is *compassionate*

Willow is *wise*

Willow *serves God*

I am Willow

She quickly sat back down and breathed a sigh of relief. *Well, I'm glad that's done with.* She glanced over at Tyler to see he was smiling at her, like *genuinely* smiling. He wasn't smirking or sneering or snickering. *He really is pretty cute.*

~~~~~~~~~~

That night after supper, Willow was mentally exhausted from everything that had happened during the school day. Mom could tell she was pretty rundown and suggested she go to bed early. For once, Willow did not object. As she drifted off to sleep, she wondered if she'd have her nightmare again. She did, but it was different in several ways.

The barn was burning behind her, the devil dogs filled the field in front of her. She held her quarterstaff at the ready, waiting for the leader of the pack to attack. In her peripheral vision, she could see someone standing beside her. She couldn't risk taking her eyes off the hellhounds but felt reassured another person stood with her, whoever it might be. The leader of the pack lunged at her and she whacked it in the head with her staff, stunning it momentarily. Another dog leapt at the person beside her, who must have had a weapon of some kind as well because she heard the beast hit the ground with a thump. Together they each took down several more, but there were just too many of them all coming at once and they were overwhelmed.

Willow awoke with a start, but she wasn't gasping for breath or drenched in sweat. Someone fought alongside her this time. She was not alone. But who was it?

6

THE FAERY FOREST

---

*"I was fascinated by fairies when
I was growing up, and I wanted
to see one dreadfully."*

~ LAURA AMY SCHLITZ ~

Over the course of the week, Willow was becoming used to her nightly dream of demon dogs. Somewhere along the way, she noticed a second figure began appearing alongside her as well but, like the first, she never had a chance to properly see who these mysterious helpers were. Although they were putting down greater numbers of attacking dogs every time, they were always eventually overwhelmed by the sheer number of the creatures.

She also hadn't really thought about Gehenna all week as there were no telltale appearances or feelings of dread indicating her presence. *Maybe she'll just go away.* It was a hopeful thought, but she doubted it would be so easy.

She began making her quarterstaff in woodworking class. After getting everyone started on the first step of making their wooden swords, Mr. O'Norscon took Willow to the other area of the woodworking classroom to show her what to do.

"The first thing you need to do is strip all the bark from the willow branch. The quickest way to do so will be using a couple of extremely sharp tools, so be careful. If you were working on a log, you'd want to use a hand axe, but since you're working on a large branch, I'll give you something a little smaller: a hatchet."

He fished around in a nearby tool cabinet and found a small hatchet. It looked *very* sharp to Willow.

"You'll want to lay the branch down on the workbench and kind of score the bark with numerous short, staccato blows." He demonstrated what he meant. "What this does is create lots of areas for the next tool to get underneath the bark when you go to shave it off. I'll check in on the sword makers while you do this first step."

Willow almost felt bad about hacking away at this piece of an ancient tree, but she was also excited to transform the big, old, gnarly branch into a beautiful, straight pole.

When Mr. O'Norscon returned, he examined Willow's work. "Well done. Now we need to hold the branch in place on the workbench for this next part, and we'll do so by using two clamp-on vises."

He retrieved two devices from the tool cabinet that were each a combination of a vise attached to a C-clamp. With the branch lying on the table, he positioned one at each end of the branch, securing the C-clamp portion to the workbench itself. He twisted a lever on the vise in the right direction to open the jaws wide enough to accept the branch, then turned the lever the opposite direction to tighten the jaws enough to hold the branch securely in place without crushing it.

"With the branch held firmly in place, you can now work the bark off the branch using—" He grabbed yet another tool from the cabinet consisting of a blade with handles on both ends set perpendicular to the blade itself, "—this handy little tool called a drawknife or wood shaver. These come in all lengths, but I think this five-inch drawknife should be just right for you. Notice how the blade is sharpened into an angle called a chisel bevel, which is what makes it so good at shaving. And the reason it's called a 'draw' knife is because you grip it with both hands, like so, and draw it toward you to shave the bark off."

Willow nodded her head with each instruction, though it was a lot to take in. Mr. O'Norscon went on, "And when you're done with the area you can comfortably get to with the branch in this position, then you just have to loosen the vises enough to rotate the branch to expose the next area you need to work on, yah? And don't over tighten the vises; you don't want to crush the ends of the branch."

This was hard work for Willow, but she felt satisfied doing it. It felt good to be crafting something with simple but effective tools she would otherwise probably never have occasion to use. She worked the bark off the first part of the willow branch and repositioned it to repeat the process. All the while, she kept an eye on the branch, continuously superimposing a straight line down its center to keep reminding herself there was a pole inside it, straight and true. The wood underneath the bark was beautiful, showing wavy patterns of cream and red swirls. The reddish tones were not unlike her own hair in the sunlight outdoors. This bark removal process took her the rest of the week, but the feeling of accomplishment was worth the effort.

~~~~~~~~~~

Much of the week was also spent preparing for the Spring Craft Fair held each year on the Saturday following spring equinox. This was the major fundraising and community event of the year, and all students and their families had roles to play in making it a success. The school always brought in a wide array of regional craftspeople to sell their hand-crafted jewelry, clothing, toys, and more. Families contributed food and baked goods to serve a light lunch. There was a raffle for various themed baskets filled with all sorts of donated items and gift certificates. The younger children got to enjoy craft activities and puppet shows. However, the single most important feature of all, at least for Willow, was always the Faery Forest set up in the woodworking classroom.

She thought about the first time she attended the craft fair when she was probably three years old. Her father bought two tickets and gave one to her so she could hand it over to the ticket-taker in the hallway as they waited for their turn.

She was filled with anticipation as she stared at the closed door before her, anxiously waiting for it to open. When the door did finally open, she held her father's hand tightly as they stepped into another world.

Before her was a winding pathway lined on both sides, floor-to-ceiling, with evergreen boughs. Twinkling white lights imparted a warm, cozy glow reminiscent of Christmastime. She saw something hiding in one of the pine boughs: a tiny, translucent crystal catching the light and reflecting it. Then she saw a pale-green faery peeking out from another spot, and then a purple crystal, and a yellow gemstone, and more faeries of every possible variety, and gnomes, and more crystals and sparkly trinkets of all colors and shapes. The faeries and gnomes were all just figurines, of course, but to her three-year-old mind that longed to believe in faeries, it was nothing short of breathtakingly magical.

Every place she looked among the boughs, she discovered something new to marvel at as they slowly explored their way along the path. She was vaguely aware of peaceful music being played. When they rounded the last bend of the path, the source of the music was revealed. A young woman dressed in flowing white robes played a small harp. She never stopped playing, but she indicated with a warm smile and twinkling eyes that Willow was to approach the pedestal between her and the angel. Upon the pedestal was a large stone basin of water, lined with moss and pebbles. On the outside edge of the basin, Willow saw seeds of various shapes, along with a small paper sailboat.

Willow somehow knew what she was supposed to do. Her father was rather perplexed by all this. She selected a seed, placed it in the boat, put the boat in the water, and blew into its tiny sail to send the boat across the water to the other side of the basin. The angel nodded her approval and indicated she was now ready to exit the Faery Forest. It was a deeply satisfying experience. Willow had walked the Faery Forest every year (except the year she was in Brazil), even after she was far older than most of the children who entered. There was a bit of magic in the Faery Forest she didn't want to give up.

Sixth-grade Willow and her classmates had been waiting all week to find out their craft fair assignments. At last, Mr. Retsof announced on Friday afternoon what everyone would be doing. There were many tasks done in pairs or trios, and those combinations would change throughout the day with each task.

"Willow, your last task of the day will be taking tickets for the Faery Forest during the last hour of the craft fair, and then Tyler will join you to disassemble it, which will probably take the two of you an hour to accomplish."

Willow was happy to have anything to do with the Faery Forest. She also didn't mind being paired with Tyler, as long as he didn't poke fun at everything she loved about it. Taking it apart at the end of the fair might also be a sad thing to do.

The Spring Craft Fair of 2016 was the first anyone could remember that took place without any snow on the ground. The warm weather brought out even more people than usual and the school building was thoroughly abuzz with activity all day long. Willow, Camille, and Luke spent an hour as a roaming trio of musicians playing tunes on their recorders. She spent another hour with Lila and Harmonie serving lunch to hungry patrons, and another hour with Brenden and Nate helping in the children's craft activity room. She was happy to get to her ticket-taking station for the Faery Forest so she could finally sit and rest.

She thoroughly enjoyed watching what the children were like as they waited their turn, and then seeing what they were like when they came out. Some were cranky at this point in the day, but they all inevitably emerged from the faery forest with a serene look of contentment on their faces. It was as if each went through some kind of transformation during their time in the Faery Forest. *There really is something magical about this.*

After an hour, the craft fair was over, and the building started emptying out. The woman playing the angel this year emerged from the Faery Forest with her little harp and went on her way. Willow waited for Tyler to appear. And waited some more.

Eventually she realized Tyler wasn't even going to show up for this final task of the day. She was more disappointed than mad. *Figures. Just when I was looking forward to being alone with him...*

She threw open the door to the Faery Forest and looked dejectedly at the gargantuan task ahead of her. She searched for the electrical outlet where the white Christmas lights should have been plugged in, but when she found it, they weren't plugged in at all; the cord just dangled near the socket. *That's weird. The lights are on, but they're not plugged in?* She searched around for another outlet but there wasn't one. *Maybe there's some kind of battery pack hidden in the evergreens or something.*

She found a large basket into which she could collect all the figurines, crystals, and other trinkets from the pine bough walls of the path. She reached for a little pink pixie figurine but somehow her hand missed it. She reached for it again and saw it *move* out of the way.

Just as she leaned in to get a closer look, the pink pixie took flight in a whir of little faery wings beating the air like a hummingbird. It hovered for a moment inches away from Willow's eyes with such a sweet smile on its tiny face. Willow's eyes were big as saucers and her mouth hung open in disbelief. Then the pink pixie flew off to some other part of the room.

More faeries of every color and shape came to life and took flight from the evergreens. Little gnomes, each about six inches in height, came leaping out of their spots in the boughs they had previously occupied. They looked like miniature grumpy old men who had been rudely awakened from a long nap, stretching and scratching themselves. Then there were the lights. They were not plugged into an outlet, and there was no hidden battery pack. Each light itself exited its bulb and flew about the room. *Tiny little flying balls of light?* Willow had no idea what those might be.

Am I dreaming this? She closed her eyes, rubbed them hard, and looked again. *Nope, still there.* The faeries and gnomes assembled before her, the balls of light hovering just above them. As one, the gnomes and faeries went down on their knees, then touched their foreheads to the ground, arms outstretched before them, and held that position. Willow remembered a vocabulary word she learned once to describe this: prostration, a way of showing respect and humility. *But why are they doing it to me?*

She was overwhelmed with emotion. She recalled the deep longing she felt as a little girl wanting to see faeries and gnomes so badly but at the same time fearing they might not be real. *But they are real. It's all real!* She promptly burst into tears. They were tears of joy, tears from years of pent-up longing, and tears of sweet release. Sometimes a tween girl just needs a good cry, and Willow was having one of those.

She stood there, mouth agape, tears streaming down her cheeks, watching in wonder as the faeries and gnomes rose up and disassembled the Faery Forest in a matter of minutes amidst the hovering orbs of light. All the boughs were stacked in neat bundles by the bulkhead stairs to be carried outside. The strings of lights were neatly wound around a large, wooden spool. The big basket had all the crystals and trinkets collected into it, along with the pebbles and seeds and paper boat from the end of the pathway. The wood and wire frames that formed the walls of the path and to which the boughs had been attached were rolled up neatly into several bundles and ready to be stored away.

It was all done, and Willow hadn't lifted a finger. She didn't know what to do or say. "Thank you, faeries. Thank you, gnomes. Thank you…lights? Thank you so much!"

The gnomes waved to her. The faeries curtsied in the air. The orbs of light vibrated in place. Then they all vanished. With no lights, the room was now dark, except for the light that spilled in from the hall through the door. Willow didn't move. She didn't want to move. She wanted to just stand there and soak in this wondrous moment forever.

"Willow?" a voice called from the hallway. It was Mr. Retsof.

"In here," Willow called back, her voice trembling with the emotion she still felt.

Mr. Retsof appeared in the doorway, flipped on the lights, and saw the state Willow was in. "Ah. I see you've met the fae folk."

"I... I..." was all she could say at first. She paused to gather her thoughts, then said, "I always wanted faeries and gnomes to be real, even more than I realized. But what are the lights?"

"Those are will-o-wisps. They are beings of pure light and are quite mysterious."

"But why haven't I seen the fae folk before? Why only now?" Willow wondered aloud.

The teacher replied matter-of-factly, "You clearly have the Gift of Sight."

Willow was caught off-guard by this. "Wait a minute, you know about my Gift of Sight?"

Mr. Retsof smiled, "I knew the moment I met you there was at least one divine gift in you, waiting to be awakened."

Willow remembered the song he'd sung to her and how it made her feel so strange. "That song you sang..."

"I also have the Gift of Sight, but music is my main divine gift. It awakens that which needs to be awakened in a person."

Willow wasn't at all surprised to find out her teacher's musical abilities were magical. There were a million things Willow wanted to know about the fae folk and divine gifts, but she was also feeling drained.

Mr. Retsof could see how tired she was. "You can go find your mother upstairs and leave if she's ready. You've worked very hard today, Willow, and your efforts are greatly appreciated." He extended his hand to her.

"Thank you, Mr. Retsof," she said as she shook his hand and tried to stifle a yawn.

During the car ride home, Willow was quieter than usual. There was so much she didn't know about the fae folk. *They were completely silent. Can't they talk? How can will-o-wisps be pure light? What do they eat?*

"I don't know about you, but I'm *exhausted*," her mother said. "It did seem like it was a very successful craft fair; more people than I've ever seen at one before."

Willow nodded in agreement as a thought struck her. "I've been coming to the craft fair practically my whole life, and this was definitely, without a doubt, the very best one of all."

Later in the evening, after mom had tucked her into bed, Willow waited a while and then slipped out of bed to sit looking out her window. The moon shined bright, illuminating everything outside in its silvery light. She was hoping to see some fae folk but looking up the road revealed nothing. *Maybe they're sleeping.*

As she turned to look down the road, her gaze landed instead on the road directly in front of the house. Her heart skipped a beat, and a chill tickled her arms. A dog stared directly up at her. The red eyes were especially prominent in the moonlight. *Are these things watching me all the time?* She wasn't as scared as she thought she might be. Maybe dreaming about these demon dogs every night made her feel less scared. *Except this isn't a dream. This thing is right there outside my house!*

A pale-blue faery flew into view, heading straight for the beast. When the faery passed in front of the dog, it snatched her out of the air, clamping its double rows of razor-sharp teeth on the poor thing with an audible crunch. The hellhound gave Willow one last look with the faery in its jaws, then trotted calmly off into the woods.

Willow sat staring at the spot where the beast had been. She was stunned. It was as if the faery didn't even know the demon dog was there or couldn't see it. Tears were streaming down her cheeks as she crawled back into bed. She felt utterly depleted and quietly cried herself to sleep.

7

APRIL FOOLS' DAY

"He that deceives me once, it's his fault, but if twice, it's my fault."

~ ITALIAN PROVERB ~

In woodworking class during the week following the Spring Craft Fair, Mr. O'Norscon said it was time to make the branch the right length for a quarterstaff.

"Traditionally," he said as he stood the branch on one end next to her, "you want a quarterstaff to be about one hand-length taller than you, and this branch is much taller than that. Put the heel of your hand firmly on the top of your head and then bend your hand at the wrist so it's sticking straight up." Using a charcoal pencil, he scraped a line around the circumference of the end of the branch. "Okay, now you can set up the workbench with the clamp-on vises, find a small hand-saw in the tool cabinet, and saw off the end of the branch where I've marked it."

When she had accomplished that task, Mr. O'Norscon explained, "Now comes the bulk of the work, which is to continue using the five-inch drawknife to shave off all the wood that's not needed to reveal the straight pole inside the branch, and you want it to be about one-and-a-half inches in diameter, or slightly less than that since your hands are on the small side. You seem to have a good eye, so use it to make sure you end up with a straight pole. Use the edge of the workbench as a rule and keep visualizing a straight line down the center of the branch and you should be fine." He also showed her how to sharpen the drawknife with a whetstone when it became dull.

Willow got started and soon realized just how much work this was going to involve. *Boy, he wasn't kidding about the "bulk" of the work. This is going to take forever!* She kept at it, though, and made good progress. As she examined her work, she could tell there would be many days ahead to complete this part of the process. At the end of each class, Mr. O'Norscon took her work-in-progress and carefully locked it away in the narrow little closet near the bulkhead exit. This always made Willow feel extra special, as if her project were so important it needed to be kept under lock and key.

~~~~~~~~~~

During Main Lesson this week, the class continued studying pollinators and the critical role they play in the web of life. A long-term study of nature preserves in Germany documented a 75 percent decline in flying insect populations over the course of nearly thirty years. Many of those insects were pollinators. Mr. Retsof handed out copies of the journal article about the German study and asked them to read it.

Willow glanced over at Luke. She could practically see the steam coming out of his ears as his brain went into overdrive to process what he was reading. Finally, he spoke up. "The level of decline documented in this study is *huge*. And yet there's been no collapse in pollination, or at least no major disruptions in the food supply chain for humans. So how can there be such a major decline with no impacts? It doesn't seem like the study tried to answer that question."

Mr. Retsof nodded. "You're right, Luke. The study itself was only concerned with documenting the precipitous decline in flying insect populations. What do you think it means?"

Luke seemed at a loss. Camille chimed in, "Maybe it means we can get by with fewer pollinators? Like, maybe there have been way more than are needed to keep things going?"

"That's certainly one possibility," Mr. Retsof said.

And that's when it hit Willow in a eureka kind of moment. She raised her hand and said, "Or maybe it really *would* matter to lose that many insects, but the pollination is still happening; it's just happening in a different way." She was thinking of the faeries. Who better to pick up the slack in pollination than little flying faeries most people can't even see?

Mr. Retsof looked at Willow and raised one eyebrow. "That's another possibility, Willow. But how do you suppose all that pollination is happening if not by the insect pollinators?"

Willow raised one eyebrow herself in response. *If he thinks I'm going to say something about faeries in front of the whole class, he's got another thing coming.* "I have no idea."

~~~~~~~~~~

Willow came to cherish the woodworking classes where she spent the entire period just shaving away more of the branch with the drawknife. It was a very rhythmical, almost meditative kind of work. Once she got the hang of the most effective and efficient way of handling the drawknife, she could get into "the zone" of the work and let her mind wander to whatever topics suited her fancy.

The conversations and laughing and general buzz of her classmates were ever-present. At first, she found it distracting because she wanted to know what was going on. It felt like she was always missing out on something as she was tucked away in a different part of the woodworking room. Eventually, she just let it go because the work before her was more important and satisfying than whatever middle school dramas were happening with her classmates. Besides, she could always catch up on any need-to-know gossip over lunch.

The words of Pastor Gayle's second sermon this past Sunday echoed in her mind. "Jesus was the ultimate example of empathy, compassion, and kindness. We are each called to treat one another, even strangers, the way Christ himself treated others." Willow was still somewhat confused about the difference between empathy and sympathy, but she knew she was empathetic. She just assumed everyone knew what it was like to understand other people's feelings as deeply as she did. But Pastor Gayle was talking about a distinct decline of empathy in society.

Her thoughts also returned to what Pastor Gayle had told her after Gehenna appeared in church during her first sermon. "Going to Hell, when it happens, is a choice." She couldn't help but wonder what happened that made Gehenna *choose* Hell. *Why? Why would someone choose Hell? It makes zero sense to me.*

On another day, she thought about her nightly dream of the demon dogs in the field. She no longer even thought of it as a nightmare since she didn't wake up in such a panic the way she did the first few times. The number of mysterious figures fighting by her side continued to expand, but they were always too blurry to identify. She wished she could figure out who these fellow fighters were.

On yet another day, Tyler wandered over. "Hey *Wee-low*, how's the *stick* coming along?"

Willow did not appreciate him interrupting her meditative work. "Well enough to kick your butt with it, that's for sure," she shot back.

With overly dramatic indignation he said, "Are you challenging *me* to a duel, *Wee-low*?"

She immediately felt a little nervous flutter in her stomach. Tyler was by far the most gifted of her classmates at anything athletic, and he was bigger than her, though not by much. "You bet I am, Tyler, and won't you be embarrassed when you get beat by a *girl*." He just gave her his trademark smirk and swaggered back to the sword-making area.

Oh boy. Now I've done it. I'm gonna have to figure out how to use this thing once I finish making it.

~~~~~~~~~~

As Willow arrived at school on Friday, she took a deep breath and steeled herself for what she knew lay ahead: April Fools' Day. In Willow's experience, the first day of April was one requiring extra vigilance. The boys in her class were known for planning any number of pranks to play on unsuspecting victims throughout the day. Willow was determined not be among their prey, mostly because Tyler would probably be the ringleader of all such pranks.

The first stop every student made before greeting their teacher and entering their classroom was their locker. At Elm City Waldorf, the lockers were built into the wall in such a way that students could access them from outside the classroom as well as inside the classroom, which was convenient when students needed to grab something during class from their locker. The lockers didn't actually lock on either side, and Willow suspected there might be some locker pranks.

She paused at the far end of the upstairs hallway to observe. Sure enough, she saw Camille open her locker only to have a whole pile of books and papers come tumbling out all over the floor. Willow rushed over and helped her pick everything up. She felt bad about how embarrassed Camille probably felt.

Camille smiled and said, "Thanks, Willow. I wasn't even thinking about what day today is. I should have known they would do something like this." The boys had obviously accessed the locker from inside the classroom, stood all the books and papers up on the shelf and then leaned them against the hallway door of the locker.

Willow had everything in her backpack so her hands were free, which meant she could greet Mr. Retsof and go into the classroom to access her locker from that side. She carefully opened her locker and saw the same arrangement. A triumphant smile spread across her face at thwarting the first attempted prank.

The boys tried to brush off the fact Willow had outsmarted them. Tyler, of course, couldn't resist saying something. "Oh darn, smarty-pants *Wee-low* didn't fall for our prank. Well, better luck next year, I guess."

Does he really think I'm that stupid? Tyler was trying to make it sound like this was the only prank they had planned for the day, but Willow certainly wasn't going to fall for that routine. She also didn't mind making them think she would be letting her guard down. Using her best acting skills, she put a look of genuine relief on her face. "Whew! Glad I don't have to worry about more pranks. Well, it was a good try." The boys were terrible at hiding their knowing glances to each other.

In woodworking class after Main Lesson, Willow finished shaving off the final layers of wood to reveal her completed quarterstaff. It turned out well, and Mr. O'Norscon praised her work. "You've done very well on this project so far, Willow, and you have just enough time to give it a light sanding and rub it down with flaxseed oil to finish it off. It should be sufficiently dry on Monday for you to start learning how to use it in preparation for a demonstration at our May Day celebration."

As she sanded the staff, Willow wondered how she would demonstrate the quarterstaff if she was the only one. The rest of the class would be doing the traditional sword dance sixth graders learn for May Day. When the sanding was finished, Willow used a soft cloth to rub the entire quarterstaff with flaxseed oil, which brought out the wood's coloring and patterns and gave the staff a soft shine.

She left woodworking feeling proud of her work and *hungry*. It was time for lunch, and everyone was planning to eat outside because it was another warm, beautiful day. Willow's lunch "box" was a stainless steel, three-tiered, pyramid-shaped tiffin. No one else in her class had a metal lunch box, but she didn't mind. She loved her tiffin, and Mom could put a surprising amount of food into it. She was looking forward to seeing what she'd be feasting on outside with the sunshine on her face. When she opened her locker, however, she discovered her tiffin was missing. She had a pretty good idea of who was behind this little prank.

Mr. Retsof had already headed downstairs with most of her classmates so he wouldn't be any help. Tyler was getting his lunch out of his own locker and said, "What's the matter, *Wee-low*? Missing something?"

Willow had no patience for this. "Okay, Tyler, very funny. I'm hungry. Where is it?"

"Where's what? I have no idea what you're talking about, *Wee-low*." He slammed his locker shut and sprinted down the hall to catch up with everyone else heading outside.

Camille was the only one left getting her lunch. She gave Willow a sympathetic look and said, "I heard the boys snickering in woodworking class about hiding your lunch box up in the attic. Do you want me to wait while you go look for it?"

Willow appreciated the offer but could tell Camille was anxious to get outside with everyone else. She also noticed Camille didn't offer to help her look for it, which she also understood. Willow would have appreciated the company as attics always creeped her out.

"No," Willow sighed, "it's all right. You go ahead and I'll see you out there. Tyler sure knows how to get on my nerves."

Camille started to leave, then turned back to Willow and quickly said, "You know it's because he likes you, right?" She ran off to join the others without waiting for an answer.

Willow hadn't considered Tyler might actually like her. It made sense, though, when she thought about it. The whole boys-teasing-girls-they-like thing because they're... What? *Immature? Clueless? All the above!*

The growling sound coming from her stomach reminded her of what she had to do now. Standing in front of the closed door of the attic stairway, Willow took a deep breath and opened the door. This was not something she wanted to do by herself, but she didn't want Tyler or the other boys to think she was afraid. The narrow stairway leading up to the attic was dark and dusty. She found a light switch and flipped it on. One lonely, bare bulb at the top of the stairs cast a dim glow to light her way. Stairs creaked and groaned with each step.

At the top of the stairs, Willow found another light switch. This one turned on another weak bulb in the center of the attic. It shed little light over the vast space crowded with all manner of random things from costumes and set pieces for plays to discarded chairs and desks to filing cabinets and who knew what else. She never realized before just how huge this room was. There were no windows to let in natural light, which made it seem all the creepier because she knew it was a bright, sunny day outside.

How am I ever going to find my tiffin in this mess? She was trying to ignore how fast her heart was beating as she began making her way through the sea of shadowy shapes and dust-covered detritus. She really wanted to get out of there and was considering just going hungry for the day, but how would she explain to Mom why she didn't have her tiffin? Just then she caught a faint glint of light, a reflection off the shiny stainless steel of her tiffin. It was in the furthest possible corner of the attic, sitting atop filing cabinets stack nearly to the ceiling, leaving just enough room for her tiffin to be carefully placed there. *How the heck did Tyler even get it up there in the first place?*

Now she had to figure out how to climb up high enough to get it down. The ceiling was at least ten feet high. She pulled open the lowest drawer of the stacked filing cabinets, thinking she could just stand on that to reach high enough. The drawer was full of what looked like past student artwork. Willow always enjoyed looking at Waldorf artwork. She lifted the stack of papers out of the drawer to take a quick peek through them but then saw something far more intriguing underneath. It was a plain, leather-bound journal with a strap around it to keep it closed. It looked very old. As much as she wanted to look inside it, the rumbling in her stomach was demanding she get her lunch.

She put the artwork back in the draw and set the journal aside. Realizing there was no way she could stand on the open drawer without tipping the whole cabinet, she looked around for other options. She ended up dragging an old school desk over and climbed atop it to reach her tiffin. As she climbed back down, she looked at the leather journal. Her curiosity was telling her to take it. Would it be wrong of her to take it? *Not if I put it back. I'm just borrowing it.* She grabbed it and ran for the attic stairs.

Willow was happy to get out of the attic as quickly as possible. After a quick stop at her locker to stuff the journal in her backpack and grab her water bottle, she headed outside to join everyone else for lunch. She also planned to give two-faced Tyler a piece of her mind, whether he liked her or not.

8

A MOONLIT CEMETERY

> *"A well-kept cemetery in the light of day can be a lovely place. A cemetery in the dark of night is no place for the living."*
>
> ~ ANONYMOUS ~

"How was school today?" Willow's dad asked when she arrived at his apartment, which was only a few blocks away from the school.

Willow plopped her backpack on the floor and flopped into the wingback chair next to his desk with a sigh. "You were a boy once, right? What is *wrong* with boys? Why are they so, I don't know, frustrating?"

Stifling a chuckle with a mock serious look he replied, "Mm. *All* boys? Or do you mean a *particular* boy?"

"I mean *all* boys, but especially Tyler. He's been super annoying lately." She could feel her cheeks getting hot.

Her dad noticed this and smiled as he said, "Maybe he *likes* you, Willow."

Camille said the same thing. Could it really be true? "Well, if that's true, and I'm *not* saying it is, then he's got a pretty dumb way of showing it."

"And that," her dad went on, "is exactly what's wrong with boys your age. But enough of this boy talk. What do you feel like for dinner tonight?"

Willow could always count on her dad to get good takeout when she overnighted with him. "How about Thai?"

"Sounds like a plan to me. Your usual? Chicken satay, steamed dumplings—"

"—And I'll have some of your pad Thai," she finished for him, which is what he always ordered if they chose Thai.

~~~~~~~~~~

Later that evening after her father had said goodnight, told her not to stay up too late, and was soon snoring away in his room, Willow retrieved the leather-bound journal from her backpack. She settled into the small recliner her father had gotten for her bedroom and put the footrest up. It was the perfect chair for reading. Her heart was thumping as she carefully undid the leather strap. She was intensely curious to see what was in it. On the inside front cover was written the name Annabel Harper. It looked as if it had been written with a fountain pen; something Willow could tell because they sometimes used fountain pens at school for special projects.

It was a diary. The first entry was dated June 28, 1886, and Annabel Harper was describing a brand-new instrument her husband had brought home from a business trip to Philadelphia. It was called an autoharp, and she was fascinated by its sound and the mechanics of how it worked. She compared it to other instruments she already played, such as the hammered dulcimer and the zither.

Several more entries on subsequent days were mostly about the joys and challenges of being a young mother. Annabel referred to her infant son as "baby Jack" in the diary, and

Willow got the impression she had started writing in this journal soon after his birth.

In early July there was an entry about how pleased she was that the construction of the Lincoln Street School (which Willow knew was the building now housing Elm City Waldorf) for grades one through six was nearly finished. Annabel had secured a promise of employment as the school's music teacher, which excited her to no end. But she also noted her husband was not exactly pleased about the arrangement.

Willow had to remind herself this was in the 1880s, a period her class had explored last fall in a history block about the industrial revolution. Most schoolteachers were probably men or unmarried women. She supposed a young mother would be expected to remain home to care for the child. Willow was impressed how Annabel's love of music and desire to teach children were strong enough to overcome what society and her own husband expected of her.

As Willow flipped through the pages of the journal, she came across an actual photograph, perfectly preserved. Willow had seen plenty of old-time black and white photographs in history books, and she was always surprised by how solemn people's expressions were, as if photographs required a very serious look on one's face.

In this photograph, however, there was a big smile on Annabel's face, though it was a close-lipped smile not showing any teeth. She was strikingly beautiful. Thick, black hair was swept up on top of her head as they did in those days, with some strands falling along her temples on either side of her head. She had perfectly arched brows, delicate features, and eyes that were so pale they looked like those of a Siberian husky.

Annabel was seated in a fancy armchair holding baby Jack in her lap, who had such a goofy, toothless grin on his face it made Willow laugh out loud. He looked ridiculous with the fancy, white gown babies often wore for photographs in those days. By contrast, the husband looked dead serious. His dark hair was severely parted on one side, and his expression was so solemn it bordered on grim. The monocle he wore on one eye didn't help, either.

Willow tucked the photograph back into the pages of the journal. She wanted to read more but her eyes were heavy, and she drifted off to sleep in the recliner. The now familiar nightmare came to her once again, but with unexpected differences.

There were at least a dozen blurry figures ready to fight alongside her. Glancing to her left, where she could just make out her willow tree, there was a group of faeries and gnomes gathered under it, cowering in fear. Willow understood in the dream that the fae folk could hear the snarling and barking of the hellhounds but could not see them. How dreadful that must be for them. She and those with her had to hold the line they formed against the hellhounds. If they failed, the demon dogs would get to the fae folk and tear them apart, just like she had seen in real life the night before. Despite her determination, when the wave of beasts surged forward, she and her fellow fighters were again overwhelmed.

Willow awoke more startled by this version of the dream than she had been in days. *The hellhounds want to destroy the fae folk? But why?*

A light shining through the blinds of the window closest to her interrupted her thoughts. She raised the shade to see a single will-o-wisp hovering just outside the window. Willow marveled at the small orb of pure, white light. It vibrated in place for a moment, then zipped off to the side out of sight. Just as Willow wished she could have more time to look at it, the will-o-wisp popped back into view. It vibrated again, then moved very slowly out of sight again, then popped back into view.

Willow was puzzled by this behavior. *It's almost like it wants me to follow it?* The will-o-wisp pulsated and vibrated, which struck Willow as a *yes*. She had no idea what time it was, but it felt like the middle of the night. She had fallen asleep in her recliner before getting ready for bed, so she was still in the clothes she'd worn to school that day. Her pulse quickened at the idea of going out in the middle of the night. This was not something she would normally ever do, but she'd also never been asked to do so and by a will-o-wisp no less. It seemed important.

Her heart was pounding in her chest as she nodded her head to the will-o-wisp and carefully began to make her way out of her bedroom. She paused in the hallway and listened. Her dad was still snoring. Willow tiptoed through the apartment to the stairs leading down to the side porch entrance, put on her sneakers, and quietly slipped out the door. The will-o-wisp came down to her level and started floating toward the street. Willow took a deep breath and followed.

The night air was crisp and chilly. Although there was only a quarter-moon high in the sky, it was bright. She followed the will-o-wisp across Roxbury Street and along Beech Street to where it ended at Beaver Street. Every house she passed was dark and all was quiet. The world was asleep. *What am I even doing out here at this hour?*

On the other side of Beaver Street was the entrance to Woodland Cemetery. The will-o-wisp proceeded through the entrance without pausing. Willow, on the other hand, did pause. In fact, she stopped short on the street side of the entrance. It was one thing to be out in the middle of the night but going into a cemetery at night was not something she wanted to do. Besides, the sign on one side of the entrance clearly said *open from dawn to dusk*. No one should be going into the cemetery in the middle of the night, although there was no gate to prevent anyone from doing so.

The will-o-wisp came back and urgently bounced up and down in the air in front her face as if to say *come on*. Looking beyond the bouncing light, Willow saw a sea of gravestones bathed in silvery moonlight, along with the massive hemlocks and oaks scattered throughout, like towering sentinels keeping a grim watch over the dead. The will-o-wisp once again crossed the entrance into the cemetery. This time Willow followed, though she wasn't at all sure this was a good idea.

There were three different cemeteries that kept growing over the decades and all joined together into one sprawling home for the dead covering many acres: Greenlawn Cemetery, Woodland Cemetery, and Woodland Northeast Cemetery. During the day, lots of people used the many paved pathways for walking, jogging, and bicycling. Willow herself had done so on plenty of occasions with her dad. It was a peaceful, lovely place in the daytime, like a giant park. At night, however, it seemed dark and foreboding.

Deep into the heart of the cemetery, she followed the will-o-wisp, whose light started to dim as Willow began to hear sounds of movement up ahead. Thin clouds drifted in front of the moon, making it harder to see. She could barely make out two figures in the distance but couldn't tell what they were doing. The will-o-wisp was only a soft glow now, and it settled in front of a simple slate headstone and vibrated. Willow crouched down with the will-o-wisp to avoid being seen by whoever was out there. The light of the will-o-wisp illuminated the carved stone before her. Willow's heart stopped when she saw the inscription on the stone.

Annabel Lee Harper
Born May 23, 1859
Died October 17, 1886

Willow wanted to think about what all this meant in relation to what she was reading in Annabel's diary. *Was Lee her middle name or her last name before she married? Why did she die only months after starting her diary?* The wispy clouds dissipated, and the moon shone brightly once again. Willow peeked around the edge of the headstone and gasped at what she saw. The two figures were closer now and engaged in battle among the tombstones. There was the unmistakable form of a heavily-veiled Gehenna in all her darkness. The other person was an old woman with long, gray hair in a loose-fitting, light-colored outfit of pants and shirt along with brown sandals. Her weapon looked like a walking stick to Willow.

The old woman whirled the stick above her head and crouched in a kind of fighting stance. Gehenna was forming darkness between her hands into a blob about the size of a basketball. With a violent, forward-thrusting motion of her hands, she sent the dark mass hurtling toward the old woman. At the last possible moment, the old woman spun to one side and the blob missed. But Gehenna already had another formed and shot it forward. This time, the old woman whipped her walking stick around and slapped the dark blob away.

Gehenna was forming and firing her black projectiles in rapid succession, one after another. The old woman twisted and turned, whirling her stick and displaying far more dexterity and acrobatic skill than could be expected from a woman of her age. As this went on, Willow could tell the old woman was beginning to tire. Gehenna, however, showed no signs of slowing down.

The old woman tripped on something and stumbled down on one knee. She also lost her grip on the walking stick, which fell to the ground slightly out of her reach. Gehenna hurled another blob of darkness, and this one struck the old woman full-on in the chest. The force of the blow sent her flying backward, slamming her into a huge oak tree's trunk with a sickening thud. The old woman crumpled to the ground and was still. Willow was sure she must be dead.

Willow's heart was pounding so hard in her chest she was afraid Gehenna would hear it. As if in response, Gehenna suddenly stiffened, alert to the presence of someone else in the cemetery. Slowly the woman in black turned in the direction where Willow was hiding. Too scared to move, Willow could only stare in horror as Gehenna's distorted voice came ripping into her brain.

"Coming here was a mistake you'll soon regret. They all think you're so special—your pastor, your teachers, even the fae folk prostrate themselves before you—but they will see soon enough how wrong they are. All I see is a little girl, scared and weak. You are nothing. My darkness will consume you in an instant."

As these words tore their way through Willow's mind, Gehenna was shaping another mass of darkness, much bigger than the ones she had hurled at the old woman. It shot forward and Willow knew this was how it would all end for her. *How will anyone know what happened to me?*

The will-o-wisp beside her sprang upward, its dim light exploding into a blaze of blinding white light like a mini supernova as it intercepted the blob of darkness mere feet from Willow. The black mass burst into a cloud of ash that drifted to the ground. The will-o-wisp was now faint, barely visible, but still hovered in front of Willow, between her and Gehenna. Out of nowhere another will-o-wisp joined it, and then another. Within a matter of seconds there was a wall of will-o-wisps, all shining brightly. It was barrier of pure white light. Gehenna hurled another dark mass. It exploded with a poof into ash when it hit the wall of light.

Gehenna let out an unholy shriek of rage and shot off like a black streak into the chilly night air. One by one the will-o-wisps floated away until only the diminished one was left. Willow hoped the poor thing wasn't permanently damaged from its heroic act to save her from Gehenna's attack. She marveled at how powerful these mysterious creatures were. Willow cupped her hands gently underneath the orb of weak light as a gesture of thanks, and then it too floated off slowly into the distance.

Willow heard a moan come from the direction of the big oak where the old woman had been struck down. She was stirring, then sat up, looking groggy and disoriented. Willow approached her cautiously and asked, "Umm, hi, are you okay?"

The old woman gave her head a shake and squinted at Willow. "I will be, eventually. I think the more relevant question is what in the world are *you* doing in a cemetery in the middle of the night?"

"Uh, I… Well, I…" Willow stammered. She wasn't sure what she should or shouldn't say. *But this woman was fighting Gehenna, so I should be able to trust her, right?* "I followed a will-o-wisp here."

"I see," the woman said, eyeing Willow up and down. "You can see the fae folk, you look to be around twelve years of age, which puts you in the sixth grade… You must be Willow."

Willow was taken aback by this. "Yes, I am, but how do you—"

The old woman raised a hand to cut her off. "That's not important right now. Fetch me my walking stick."

Willow quickly retrieved the stick and handed it to her. With difficulty, she used it to pull herself into a standing position. "Ah, that's better. Now, the most important thing for you is to go home straightaway. You and I will see each other again soon. Now go!"

Willow ran the whole way back to her father's apartment. After pausing at the side porch entrance long enough to catch her breath, she quietly made her way to her room, got into her pajamas, and crawled into bed. *Who was this old woman who fought Gehenna? What did Gehenna mean about people thinking I'm special?* These and many other questions swirled around in her mind without answers until she finally drifted off to sleep.

9

TREES AND TRAINING

> *"Notice that the stiffest tree is most easily cracked, while the bamboo or willow survives by bending with the wind."*
>
> ~ BRUCE LEE ~

When Willow walked into the classroom Monday morning, she was pleased to see new chalk art adorning the right-most quadrant of the blackboard, especially since it was a very detailed presentation of a willow tree that looked a lot like the willow tree outside her home.

After going through the usual morning routines and rituals, Mr. Retsof kicked off Main Lesson with an intriguing question: "Do trees communicate?" He let that question sink in for a good long time. Willow glanced around at her classmates. No one was going to offer up an answer with any kind of confidence because no one wanted to look foolish if their opinion turned out to be wrong or different from what most were thinking.

Why are we always so obsessed with not wanting to look stupid? We don't offer any opinion on anything at all, waiting to hear what others will say first. It's just stupid, but she certainly wasn't going to say anything first, either.

The scoffing expression on Tyler's face said, "no way," though he wasn't saying it out loud. Harmonie was considering the possibility of tree communication. Luke was looking pretty skeptical as well. Everyone else looked generally clueless.

"Since no one's willing to venture an answer to that question, I'd like you to listen to a podcast episode that does provide an answer; one that some of you will no doubt find surprising. This comes from a twelve-minute episode of the *Wow in the World* science podcast. Give it a listen and then we'll discuss it." He pressed play on a tape recorder sitting on his desk. Willow only knew what it was because her mom had an old one at the house she used to play with as a young child.

Willow listened with interest about a woman scientist who proved trees do communicate with each other. The details of her experiment were a bit baffling, but she understood the general gist of what she figured out, and it was incredible.

Trees *do* communicate with each other, and the way they communicate is through a vast underground network of fungal threads running through forest soil. These fungal threads intertwine with the roots of trees. If something threatens one tree, such as an invasive insect, the tree sends enzyme signals down through its roots and through the fungal network to alert other trees nearby. Those trees respond by upping whatever defense mechanisms they have against the attack. And the trees don't just communicate between individuals of their own species; they communicate *across* species.

Even more incredible is how they *help* each other. If there's a young tree sapling struggling to get enough sunlight because of the surrounding trees blocking the sun, then trees of all species around it will send it extra nutrients. This flies in the face of the typical Darwinian "survival of the fittest" framework most people see when they look at a forest. They see a bunch of trees all competing against each other for resources. The woman scientist, however, showed how trees are communicating in order to *cooperate.* Trees are collaborating to make the forest ecosystem healthy for all of them.

When the recording was finished, everyone sat in silence. Mr. Retsof patiently waited for someone to say something. Eventually, it was Luke who spoke up. "The experiments the scientist did to confirm inter-species communication between trees was impressive. Turning the idea of forest competition into forest *cooperation* is fascinating. The one thing I don't understand, though, is the fungal threads. I get the role they're playing, but I don't understand *why* they do it. What's in it for them, like from an evolutionary biology perspective?" Willow was always impressed with Luke's ability to put words to things she was thinking about but didn't know how to say.

"That's an excellent follow-up question, Luke, and one I don't have an immediate answer to, honestly. There are many features in nature that, to me, point to the intentional design of a Creator, though just as many people, if not more, don't see it that way. But your question does get at an interesting area to explore when it comes to the lives of plants and other non-animal organisms. You asked what's in it for the fungal threads, as if they could choose to *not* facilitate communication among the trees. But I don't think they can make such a choice any more than a flower could choose not to bloom, or a bee could choose not to collect pollen. They do what they naturally do in order to stay alive."

Willow's brain was beginning to hurt from trying to sort out these complicated ideas. She was relieved when Mr. Retsof finished Main Lesson early because he had something special to present to the class. He disappeared into his teacher's closet and emerged carrying what looked like a large wooden trunk with handles on either side. But it wasn't a trunk with a lid that opened. It was a cabinet with drawers. He set it atop his own desk. The wood was lacquered black, and the drawers had geometric shapes carved into them. Each drawer also had a white, ceramic pull with black roman numerals painted on its face.

"This is my *Wunderkammer,* or cabinet of wonders. There are sixteen numbered drawers. In each drawer is something special I have chosen for you to add to your weapon during woodworking class today. As I call your name and number, come retrieve the item out of your drawer, take it with you, and go down to the woodworking room. Mr. O'Norscon is expecting you a bit early today. Brenden, you are first, so drawer number one is for you."

Brenden walked up to the *Wunderkammer,* pulled open the drawer numbered I, reached in and drew out a sizable, dark-red, elliptical gemstone, flat on one side. "Whoa! This is going to be *awesome.*" He hurried out of the classroom, clearly eager to add this embellishment to his sword. Bridget was next and she pulled out a pale-blue, diamond-shaped gemstone. One by one, each student was called to retrieve their treasure, each one a unique gemstone to be added to the hilt of their sword. *Looks like I'll be last yet again.* She didn't mind. She just wondered what would be in her drawer.

It was finally Tyler's turn, which meant Willow would be next. Tyler whipped open his drawer rather unceremoniously and yanked out a shiny, rectangular stone as black as midnight. Mr. Retsof said, "That's obsidian, Tyler, which is basically volcanic glass formed from rapidly cooled lava. That particular piece came from the Newberry Volcano in

Oregon." Tyler's eyes lit up as he marched triumphantly out of the classroom.

Finally, it was just Willow and Mr. Retsof in the classroom. "Okay, Willow, your turn."

By this time, the anticipation had grown to such a fevered pitch her hand trembled as she reached for drawer number XVI. She pulled it out carefully, only to see it was completely empty. "Um… There's nothing in here, Mr. Retsof." *Talk about building up to a big letdown.* Willow was crestfallen.

"Ah yes, sorry about that, Willow. I needed to speak with you privately about your unique situation, and here we are. What I believe will work best for your quarterstaff is something much more than a small gemstone. What that might be I have no idea, but you must find it yourself. I suggest an exploration of the forest behind your house. Just be open to whatever guidance comes your way."

Willow's disappointment instantly turned to joy. *A quest! I have to go on a quest to find the treasure for my quarterstaff. How cool is that?* "Yes! I can definitely do that. I'll do it this weekend for sure!"

~~~~~~~~~~

Movement Class at Elm City Waldorf School was the equivalent of physical education or gym class in other schools. Today was the day for Willow's classmates to begin learning the sword dance sixth graders traditionally perform at the school-wide May Day celebration. *How is this going to work if I'm the only one with a quarterstaff?* Willow had already attended her fair share of May Day events and had seen the sword dances of sixth graders. At various points during the dance, the swords are interlocked in such a way as to form a star one of the dancers raises over their head as the group continues marching a circular path. There was no way a quarterstaff could be worked into that mix.

Weapons in hand, Mr. Retsof led the class outside to the playground. Leaning against the wooden fence that bordered one side of the playground was an older woman with a walking stick. Willow gasped as she recognized her as the old woman who had fought with Gehenna in the cemetery. "Okay everyone, you might recognize Dr. Sosserie," gesturing to the old woman, "who normally teaches the sword dance. But this year I'll be teaching you the sword dance while Dr. Sosserie works with Willow on her quarterstaff demonstration."

Great. Yet another thing that singles me out. She was getting tired of always being the odd one out. Dr. Sosserie motioned for Willow to follow her. They were heading to upper yard where the younger children have recess and Games Class, which is outdoor gym class for the younger grades. Willow couldn't help but notice how Dr. Sosserie walked with a distinct limp. *Is that from her battle with Gehenna? What kind of doctor teaches sword dances and quarterstaff demonstrations to middle school kids? And she's so…old.*

Once they climbed the short embankment to the upper yard, Dr. Sosserie turned to her with a twinkle in her eye and a somewhat crooked smile on her lips and said, "Am I old? Yes. But I still have a good deal of fight left in me. How much did you see in the cemetery the other night?"

"I saw it all, or at least most of it," Willow replied. "You were…amazing."

Leaning on her walking stick, Dr. Sosserie snorted in way that might have been a kind of laugh. "And yet I lost that battle. I do not intend to lose again. Now, go stand over there about four yards away from me." Willow did as instructed. "And now, throw your staff at me, however you want." Willow hesitated. Dr. Sosserie's expression changed quickly to one of impatience. "Come child, I do not have time to waste on your hesitation. Do it!"

Willow haphazardly threw her quarterstaff directly at an old, lame woman, which just felt wrong to her on so many levels. But Dr. Sosserie caught it effortlessly with her free hand, despite the strange angle of its trajectory toward her. "This is well-made, Willow. Balance is everything when it comes to mastering the quarterstaff, beginning with the staff itself, and then you as its wielder."

Without warning, Dr. Sosserie hurled the staff back at Willow. *It's weird how so many thoughts can flash through my mind in less than a second. Like this quarterstaff that's about to totally hit me in the face. I wonder if I'll have to get stitches. I've never even been to the hospital, well except the day I was born, I guess.* Reflexively, without even thinking about it, Willow caught her staff, whirled it about above her head several times and then found herself in what she could only assume was some kind of fighting stance, crouched low with her staff held in both hands horizontally before her. She stayed in that stance, frozen and wide-eyed, staring at Dr. Sosserie. The doctor's expression was both surprised and pleased in equal parts.

"What—" Willow stammered, "what just happened?"

"You, child, have the God-given Gift of *Fight*," Dr. Sosserie replied matter-of-factly, then half-muttered, "And it's a good thing or you'd probably be on your way to the hospital to get stitches…"

For her part, Willow was close to being overwhelmed by all this and promptly plopped down on the ground. She was on the verge of tears. "But Dr. Sosserie, I don't know the first thing about fighting."

Dr. Sosserie joined her on the ground, with some effort. "That's the beauty of the Gift of Fight. It fills in a lot of skill gaps early on, which allows you to get by. But as you train and gain skills, the gift boosts everything you learn to a higher level. I understand you're a dancer?" Willow nodded. "That's good. The kind of balance and poise you learn in ballet will come in handy, as will the kinds of moves you do in your Modern classes. Even your Hip Hop classes will have their use." With a chuckle she added, "I'm glad you don't take Tap classes: they're useless."

How does she know about all the dance classes I take? And how can such an old, lame woman move the way she did when I saw her fighting Gehenna in the cemetery or when I threw my staff at her?

As if in reply, Dr. Sosserie offered, "I have the Gift of Fight myself, among others, which can keep even a lame, old woman like me in good enough shape to do some damage when I need to."

"You have other gifts?" Willow asked.

"Indeed I do," the old woman replied. "Like you, I also have the Gift of Sight. Having a third gift is rare, but I have been blessed with one, which is the Gift of Telepathy: mind-reading to a certain extent, but mostly communicating telepathically."

Well, that explains a lot, but this is all crazy! Out loud she said, "I still don't really see myself as fighter. It's, I don't know, it's just not my thing, you know?"

Dr. Sosserie's voice took on a very no-nonsense tone as she said, "Doesn't matter. When you've got a God-given gift, or two, or better yet, three, you use them to serve God, plain and simple, end of story."

There wasn't really anything to say to that, so Willow gave the doctor a half-hearted smile and said, "Uh, okay?"

I'll go along with this for now, but I just don't see the point of trying to train me as some kind of warrior.

"Good," Dr. Sosserie said, using her walking stick to get up off the ground. "Let's begin."

When Willow stood up, Dr. Sosserie bowed to her slightly, so Willow gave her a bow as well.

"When I threw your staff back, you caught it, spun it around above your head and then assumed a fighting stance. I want you to try doing that again."

The doctor took Willow's staff from her, moved back several paces, and then tossed it at her, considerably less forcefully than before. Willow assumed the gift would kick in and she'd be able to repeat what she did before. Instead, she misjudged both the trajectory of the staff and the direction of her reach to catch it. The staff hit the back of her wrist, causing her to wince as a sharp pain shot up through her arm. *"Ow!"* she cried out, cradling her wrist. The staff lay on the ground before her.

The old woman didn't acknowledge her pain. Instead, she said, "Pick the staff up and try to twirl it above your head as you did before and then assume that fighting stance."

Despite her throbbing wrist, she picked up the staff and tried to spin it around above her as before. Rather than a graceful twirl, she managed to whack herself in the head with it. *"Ow!"* She tried to end up in that crouching fighting stance, but it was all wrong. She lost her balance and fell backward onto her behind with a final *"Ow!"*

Utterly confused, she could feel tears welling up in her eyes. *Some gift. This sucks.*

The doctor stood over her. "What you did before was just your gift making itself known, letting you know it will be there when you need it most. It will enhance your natural abilities, and it will boost the mastery you achieve through training. The more effort you put into learning, the more the gift will respond. Do you understand?"

Boy do I. No free superpowers. Got it. "Yes, I understand," she replied, rubbing her wrist and the side of her head. *This is going to be painful.*

Dr. Sosserie went on, "There are two main styles of quarterstaff handling with which I am familiar: the English approach and the Thai approach. I find the English approach clunky and inelegant, which wouldn't pair well with your dance training, so we'll mostly focus on the Thai approach."

"What makes the English approach clunky?" Willow asked out of curiosity.

"First, there's the grip. In the Middle Ages, an English foot soldier armed with a quarterstaff would place one hand, the 'back hand,' about a hand's breadth from the butt end of the staff and the other hand twelve-to-eighteen inches above it, not quite at the mid-point but close to it. Face me but stand sideways. If your right hand is the back hand, then you'd have your left leg toward me and your right leg back with your back hand."

Willow did so and immediately felt slightly unbalanced. "This feels…awkward."

"Exactly," Dr. Sosserie nodded in agreement. "However, one of the moves the English approach is good for are darts, which is a kind of thrusting or jabbing move. You step forward with your left leg while releasing your left-hand grip and thrusting the staff forward with your back hand."

Willow attempted such a thrust, but as soon as she jabbed the staff forward, its tip then just fell to the ground as she was then only holding it in with her back hand at the butt end. "Oh, that seems…unhelpful."

The doctor explained, "Well, if you were in an actual battle your dart would either hit your opponent, or if you missed then you'd yank the staff back so quickly to you you'd be able to grab it again with your left hand before the tip had a chance to fall."

"Gotcha. That makes sense."

"The bigger issue with the English approach," Dr. Sosserie went on, "at least for you, would be the striking blows. This is accomplished by raising the tip up and bringing it down hard on your opponent, either straight on or at an angle. But I don't think you have the arm strength to make such blows effective."

Willow tried a few such moves and had to agree. She would not be delivering any crushing blows using the English approach. In fact, "crushing blows" was not a phrase she ever thought she would be thinking about. *I'm better at talking to people than fighting them.*

"In the Thai approach," the doctor was saying, "the grip is more balanced, with your hands an equal distance apart from the mid-point, the exact distance of which depends on what feels right for you. This allows you to do much more elegant moves in terms of twirling and whirling the staff like a giant baton."

Willow gripped her staff that way, adjusting her hands a couple of times to find what felt right, and it did feel much better than the English grip. "Oh, yeah, like Darth Maul in *The Phantom Menace.*"

"Except your weapon is not quite as technologically advanced as a double-bladed light saber, nor does it need to be."

Willow was surprised Dr. Sosserie knew the *Star Wars* reference.

The doctor went on, "I've seen a well-trained quarterstaff warrior take on and beat as many as five sword fighters at the same time. I'm not saying you need to achieve that level of mastery, but we want you to put on an impressive demonstration at May Day, and the skills could come in handy down the road. But I believe movement class is already ending for today, so we'd best rejoin the others."

She bowed to Willow who returned a bow. The doctor turned and began making her way back down to the school.

Willow followed behind the doctor, her mind racing with a jumble of thoughts. *Sight. Fight. Telepathy. Awakening. How many different gifts are there? Do I have a third gift, too? How would I find out? Do I even want another gift? I'm the least likely person in the world to be a fighter, but I've got this Gift of Fight? Honestly, I don't know what God is thinking with this one. Seriously.*

~~~~~~~~~~

That night, after Mom kissed her goodnight, she retrieved the diary of Annabel Harper from its hiding place in her closet. She wanted to see what was happening in her life that would lead up to her death in October of 1886. In late August, the Lincoln Street School opened, and Annabel was fully in her element. The sheer joy she expressed in her journal entries about teaching children to sing and play simple instruments was heartwarming.

She taught the children to sing using the solfège system, just like the character of Maria in *The Sound of Music* movie taught the Von Trapp children to sing the "Do-Re-Mi" song, though without the extra bits about each note being related to real things. She had small, wooden xylophones made by a local woodworker the children loved to play, though her husband frowned at the expense as the school was just starting out and didn't have funds to reimburse her for the costs involved. Willow also got the impression Annabel's husband was a successful businessman and could easily afford such indulgences. Annabel's beauty was such that Willow imagined the woman could win her husband over to anything she wanted, despite his stern looks.

She found no clues yet as to what would happen to her, and Willow was getting sleepy. She returned the journal to its hiding place.

Apprehensively, she glanced out her window. No demon dogs were staring at her, and no will-o-wisps were tempting her to go on another nighttime adventure. With a sigh of deep relief, she crawled back into bed. The bad dream she had after falling asleep, however, was another story.

Willow and her fellow fighters formed a line along the side of the burning barn to protect the fae folk gathered under her willow tree. Her quarterstaff was different. On the top end was a pale-green crystal of some sort. She wondered where it had come from but had no time to think about it as the battle against the beasts began. She and her fellow warriors held the line.

As she whirled her staff and struck down hellhound after hellhound, she could see a different kind of movement at the far end of the hayfield. A cloud of darkness came floating out of the woods into the midst of the writhing mass of devil dogs. The darkness coalesced into the form of Gehenna. She seemed even more intimidating than when Willow first saw her in church. Gehenna raised her arms high and thrust them forward. The horde of hellhounds surged forward as one giant wave...

Willow awoke gripped with fear. Gehenna was the one directing the attack of the hellhounds.

10

A FOREST QUEST

---

*"The clearest way into the Universe
is through a forest wilderness."*

~ JOHN MUIR ~

I don't even know what I'm looking for. How am I supposed to find the right thing when I have no idea what the right thing might be? Willow stood in the backyard looking at the forest she was about to enter. She'd gone on many a walk in these woods by herself, but a fluttering in her stomach had her feeling less sure about it this time. The forest seemed darker and more foreboding than it had on her previous walks. The trees were mostly mature hemlock and spruce forming a dense wall before her. She wondered what they might be saying to each other about her.

Earlier it seemed like the perfect day for a quest, bright and sunny. Mom was off running errands and grocery shopping and probably wouldn't be back until at least lunch time. Willow had written a note saying she was going for a walk in the woods and left it on the kitchen counter so Mom wouldn't be worried if she returned home and found the house empty.

Donning her rain boots, a light jacket, and grabbing her quarterstaff, she had walked out to the back yard. There she stood, not quite sure why she was hesitating.

Closing her eyes, she took several deep breaths to calm her jitters. When she opened them, she was startled to find a gnome looking up at her. He had a short, white beard, no mustache, dark green pants, yellow shirt, soft leather boots, and a pointy, forest-green cap whose tip flopped over to one side. Unlike most of the gnomes she had encountered in the faery forest at the craft fair, she could clearly see this one's eyes, which were a dull-yellow.

The gnome then fell to his knees and prostrated himself before Willow, just like the gnomes and faeries had done at the craft fair. She found this embarrassing because she didn't know how to respond. *Why do they do this? I don't even know what it means.* Hesitantly, Willow finally spoke up: "Um… Hello?"

The gnome quickly got to his feet and raised one hand in a gesture of greeting, then nothing. Willow wished these gnomes could speak out loud. "I'm, uh, going into the forest to find something for my quarterstaff, but I don't even know what I'm looking for. Do you…maybe…want to go with me?" With the barest hint of a smile the gnome nodded his head once, did an about-face and marched into the forest. "Well, I guess that settles that," Willow murmured to herself as she followed behind the gnome. The dark wall of trees at the forest's edge gave way to less densely packed evergreens with the occasional deciduous tree in the mix, though the canopy was too high up for Willow to even see their leaves.

The gnome seemed to know where he wanted to go as he marched along, but being less than six inches tall meant each of his tiny strides didn't cover much ground.

Willow felt more like she was meandering than questing. "I'm Willow, by the way," she said aloud. "I wonder what your name is." She felt silly even saying it knowing gnomes don't speak, but she was curious. The gnome stopped and turned to look up at her with a thoughtful expression. With his right hand, he tugged twice at his right ear lobe. Willow was puzzled for a moment until she recalled all the times she had played charades, a favorite game at many a cast party after closing the production of a play or musical. "Oh! Sounds like…" she said.

The gnome looked around for a moment. He marched over to where the decaying trunk of a tree had fallen long ago but never reached the ground and was leaning against the trunk of a large hemlock. He pushed against the leaning tree trunk, but it didn't budge. Did he want to push it off the hemlock so it would fall? Willow joined him and together they pushed hard enough to complete its long-ago interrupted fall. It hit the ground with a distinctive *whump!*

Willow had her clue. "Sounds like…whump? Hm… Let's see. How about Thwump?" The gnome shook his head no. "Okay, what about Jump?" He shook his head again. "Lump?" Another no, this time with a look that conveyed impatience. Willow couldn't help but giggle a little. She was on a quest in a forest and playing charades with a gnome! The gnome, however, did not seem amused. She decided to put a little method into this madness by starting at the beginning of the alphabet to work her way through the consonants. "Bwump?" No. "Cwump?" No. "Dwump?" No. This was getting ridiculous. "Fwump?" No. "Gwump?" The little gnome nodded his head vigorously with a smile of relief. "Gwump? Your name is Gwump?" Willow shouted in delight, "Well hello there, *Gwump*! Pleased to meet you!"

Gwump again raised his hand in a gesture of greeting. Then turned and marched off in the direction they had previously been going. Willow spoke up again with an idea to cover more ground at a faster pace. "You know, Gwump, I have this pocket up here on my jacket you could ride in and just point in the direction you want me to go." He turned and looked up at her and the breast pocket of her jacket, cocking his head to one side as he considered her proposal. He nodded his head once in consent. Willow reached down, picked him up, and put him in the pocket. Most of his torso was above the top of the pocket and his arms were free to hang onto the pocket's top edge as needed. He pointed in the direction he wanted Willow to go and off they went. Willow giggled again at the sheer absurdity of what she was doing. She had a gnome named Gwump in her pocket!

After a while, they arrived at the stream running through this portion of the woods. Its origin was a spring at the apple orchard where Old Gilsum Hill Road ended, about a half-mile further up from Willow's house. It was much too wide for her to jump across.

A blood-curdling howl from behind them made the hair on the back of her neck stand up. Another sounded from a slightly different direction, also from behind them. Willow was not ready to face multiple hellhounds. She glanced down at Gwump, who was trembling in fear. He pointed frantically at her quarterstaff.

Willow shook her head and said, "No, I can't fight them with this. I don't even know how to use it yet."

This time it was Gwump who shook his head no. He pointed again at the staff and then traced an arc in the air with one hand.

Now she understood what he was trying to say. "Oh! You want me to use my staff as a kind of pole-vault-thingy. Good thinking, Gwump!"

This was not the kind of physical feat Willow would have normally attempted, but if devil dogs were coming to get them, she was ready to try anything. What if Gehenna was with them? She quickly backed up a dozen paces or so to get a running start. "Okay, Gwump, you better hang on tight!" The trembling gnome gripped the top edge of the pocket and wiggled more of himself down inside to avoid falling out.

Willow started sprinting toward the stream. She held the staff on her right side, much like she had seen pole vaulters do on television. As she got closer to the stream, her eyes focused in on a good place to plant the bottom of the staff. She was worried it might slip and they'd end up in the stream. She noticed what looked like the top of a mostly-buried boulder at the stream's edge and decided at the last minute to jam the bottom of the staff against it as a backstop. Up into the air they went, sailing over the stream in a high arc. She maintained a firm grip on the staff to make sure it came along with her.

A lot can happen in the space of a few seconds. At the apex of their trajectory, it occurred to her she hadn't really thought about the landing part of this little feat, and they were a lot higher up than she thought they'd be. She also hadn't really looked at what was on the other side of the stream where they'd be landing. Looking down gave rise to a wave of panic as all she saw was a jumble of rocks.

Willow wondered how many quests were cut short by dumb mistakes like the one she was in the process of making. She also thought this would be the perfect time for a divine gift of flying to show itself…but no such luck. They almost cleared the rocks, but not quite. At the last second, she jettisoned her staff off to one side to get it out of the way. Her feet hit the ground hard, her left foot landing squarely on a rock and her right foot landing on dirt. Pain shot up through her left ankle as she tucked into a right-side roll and hoped Gwump wouldn't be crushed in the process.

Willow sat up quickly, breathing hard. She glanced down and saw Gwump poking his head up out of the pocket, a bit wide-eyed. "You okay, Gwump?" she asked. He nodded and raised his eyebrows as if to inquire if she were okay as well. Her ankle was throbbing, but not as badly as she expected. She grabbed her staff from where it landed and started running in the direction Gwump pointed. There were more howls coming from behind them, and they were getting closer. *If they can jump the stream, we're in big trouble.*

Willow stopped short when they came to a sharp-rising embankment that led further up to a large hillside. Willow took one look at it and said, "There's no way I can climb that!" Gwump raised a hand to cut her off. He climbed out of her pocket and dropped to the ground. Standing before the bank, he made a series of curious gestures. Willow stared in disbelief as one area of the bank became blurry and then refocused into a wide, arched wooden door set into the side of the hill. It was human-height and looked like it had been there for a very long time. It creaked and groaned as it swung open in an outward direction. They dove inside and the door slammed shut of its own accord.

The howls of the demon dogs grew closer. They could hear their muffled snarling and barking outside the heavy door. Eventually the sounds faded and all was silent. They were safe. Scared and breathless, but safe.

They were in some kind of old mine shaft. Gnome-sized wall torches illuminated the tunnel before them that bent off around a corner to the right. A half-dozen gnomes came scurrying out from that direction and assembled in a half-circle around Gwump. Some of the new arrivals frowned and gestured at Willow, as if Gwump shouldn't have brought her here. Gwump made a series of pleading gestures that seemed to convince them otherwise.

As a group, they faced Willow and then prostrated themselves before her. *Again with the prostration? What am I supposed to do in response?* Not knowing what else to do, she cleared her throat and curtsied somewhat awkwardly.

The gnomes stood up and then marched off down the tunnel with Gwump at the end of the line, gesturing at Willow to follow him. They wound their way along the twisting and turning mine shaft deeper into the side of the hill. After what felt to Willow like a long time of walking at gnome-pace, the tunnel opened up into a surprisingly large cavern with several other tunnels leading off in different directions. It was a beehive of activity with dozens of gnomes coming and going from the different passages and doing different things.

A group was working in what appeared to be a kind of blacksmith area where they made objects of metal. Others seemed to work with various crystals and minerals. It wasn't at all clear to Willow what any of this was for. *Maybe it's just what gnomes did to pass the time.*

The gnome in the front of their party raised a hand and all activity immediately ceased. The gnomes gathered around in the center of the cavern to see what was happening. They were all looking at Willow, pointing at her and gesturing to each other in what appeared to be a lively conversation about her. She noticed the lead gnome was ever so slightly taller than the rest. He wore a longer shirt, bright red, around which was a black leather belt. These were the only indications he was their leader.

It suddenly occurred to her every gnome she'd seen thus far was male. She hadn't seen any female gnomes. Thinking back to the faery forest, she also realized all the faeries were female, or at least looked feminine to her. The will-o-wisps, on the other hand, were a mystery since they were just little balls of pure light. She wasn't sure what to make of all this except to wonder in her mind how gnomes and faeries and will-o-wisps made more of themselves if there weren't both males and females.

The meeting finally ended with general nods of agreement rippling through the crowd of gnomes. They had apparently reached a consensus about something. Their assembly parted as two gnomes came forward bearing what for them was a large wooden trunk. They set it down in front of Willow and opened the lid. Inside was a large crystal, nearly translucent but with a pale-green hue. One end formed a roughly circular base and from there the crystal tapered in a more-or-less triangular shape with a rounded tip. It was beautiful. She remembered seeing this crystal on her staff in last night's dream! *Does this mean my dreams are showing me the future?* This was something she really wanted to figure out, but now wasn't the time.

In her dream, the crystal was somehow attached to the top end. But how? As if in reply, the lead gnome removed the crystal from the trunk and motioned Willow to bring the tip of her staff down to his level. He showed how closely the circular based matched the diameter of her staff, being only slightly bigger in diameter. The he used one hand to make motions as if he were hollowing out the base of the crystal. Willow understood and said, "I see what you mean. You want to hollow it out so it fits over the end of the staff!" The lead gnome nodded his head.

Most of the gnomes returned to their previous tasks except for a handful who stayed to work on this special project. Using tiny little hammers and chisels of various shapes and sizes, they carefully chinked away at the base to hollow out enough of it to fit over the end of the staff by a good two inches. They sized it up against the staff several times along the way to ensure it would come out right. After the hollowing out was completed, two of the blacksmith gnomes appeared with a very rudimentary weighing scale: the old-fashioned kind with two shallow pans suspended from either end of a horizontal rod. They placed the modified crystal in one pan and kept adding small stones to the other pan until they balanced out. They returned the crystal and took their scale back to the blacksmith shop. Willow had no idea what they were up to.

Two other gnomes who had been working with a mortar and pestle appeared with some kind of substance they had made. When they started brushing it onto the top two inches of the quarterstaff and inside the hollowed-out base of the crystal, Willow realized it must be a sort of adhesive. The gnomes indicated Willow would be the one to work the crystal into place because the gnomes simply weren't strong enough to do it.

One of the gnomes handed her a thick square of soft leather. Willow's puzzled expression made the gnome sigh and roll his eyes. He mimed laying it over the crystal. It took her a minute to figure it out, but finally realized she'd have to push hard to get the crystal on the tip of the staff. The leather would prevent her from cutting herself. The two gnomes applied the mystery adhesive to the staff and inside the crystal's hollowed-out base. They then held it in place for Willow to put the crystal on it. It was a tight fit, but she managed to work it all the way onto the staff. It was perfect.

"Gosh, thank you, everyone!" Willow announced with appreciation. But the lead gnome raised his index finger, indicating they weren't done yet. He held his arms out to his sides as if he were walking on a tightrope and pretended to lose his balance. This time Willow knew exactly what the gnome meant. With the addition of the crystal, the staff was unbalanced. It needed a counterweight at the other end.

This is what the blacksmith gnomes were up to. They reappeared with a cast iron sheath to go on the bottom of the staff to counterbalance the crystal at the top. They held the iron piece in place while Willow worked the bottom end of the staff into it. She had to bang it on the floor to get it all the way on. Testing the balance of the staff, Willow could tell it was just right.

All the gnomes assembled again in the center of the cavern to bid farewell to Willow. They all bowed low but didn't do the full prostration position Willow found so perplexing.

With deep appreciation, she bowed back and said, "Thank you all so much. This means the world to me." Gwump tugged at the leg of her pants and pointed to her pocket with a smile. Apparently, he intended to accompany her on the journey back. As they entered the tunnel leading back to the mine's entrance, Willow turned back to see the gnomes waving a silent goodbye. She wondered if she would ever have occasion to come back here.

Willow and Gwump emerged from the mine and remained alert for hellhounds. All was quiet. When they came to the stream again, this time Willow opted to walk upstream to find a different way to cross. No more pole vaulting for her!

They found a spot where a tree had fallen across the stream to form a natural bridge.

When they emerged from the woods into the backyard of her house, Willow took Gwump out of her pocket and put him on the ground. "Gwump, I don't know what to say except thank you. Without you I would have wandered the woods for who knows how long. You knew exactly where I needed to go and took me there. Thank you."

Gwump gave her a happy smile and a little half-bow, then marched off into the tiered gardens that took up one entire end of the backyard, disappearing into one of the rock walls. Once again Willow found herself giggling with delight. *Gwump is a garden gnome!*

She was feeling a deep sense of peace and contentment at having successfully completed a true quest, even though it only lasted maybe a couple hours. And she was hungry! She came into the house to find Mom just putting out a hearty lunch of soup and sandwiches on the table. She saw Willow's staff and immediately remarked, "Where in the world did you ever find a fluorite crystal that large?"

Willow hadn't anticipated Mom would obviously wonder about this addition to her staff. She couldn't exactly tell her it came from a secret mine occupied by gnomes. "Oh, uh, I guess I forgot to mention this before, but Mr. Retsof has a *Wunderkammer*—a cabinet of wonders—and we each got to pick something out of it to go with our weapon. I just hadn't put it on yet. I didn't even know it was called fluorite."

"Yes, it's a mineral found in a lot of different parts of the world and in every color imaginable," Mom explained, "but the fluorite found around here is always pale-green."

Willow sometimes forgot her mom had majored in environmental studies in both college and graduate school, so she knew quite a bit about the natural world. "You know, Bonnie, who your father and I bought this house from, used to talk about some kind of old mine back in the woods somewhere. She always said it was a gold mine, but if it does exist, I think it would probably be a fluorite mine. No one's ever found it, though. What a lovely addition to your staff!"

Willow sat down at the dining table and attacked her sandwich as if she hadn't eaten in days. *Questing is hard work!*

Lying in bed later that evening, she replayed the day's adventure in her mind. Her mental playback, however, was interrupted by a soft voice deep in the recesses of her mind. Willow was sure she knew this voice. It felt familiar and safe even while it spoke a foreboding message: "Darkness is coming."

11

THE MEDIEVAL CEREMONY

"Defend the weak, protect both young and old, never desert your friends. Give justice to all, be fearless in battle and always ready to defend the right."

~ BRIAN JACQUES (SNOWSTRIPE IN *LORD BROCKTREE*) ~

Willow was having difficulty paying attention in church because she was thinking about other things. She replayed the events of her quest in her mind and wondered how Gwump spent his days. She thought about Annabel Harper and wanted to read more of her story. She tried to envision what the Medieval Ceremony would be like later in the day. The words she heard in her head the night before kept echoing her mind: "Darkness is coming."

Pastor Gayle was preaching a sermon based on "The Judgment of the Nations" passage attributed to Jesus in the Gospel of Matthew, chapter 15, verses 31–46, in which he talks about feeding the hungry, giving drink to the thirsty, clothing the naked, tending to the sick, and visiting the imprisoned. At the judgment day, those who did these things would be blessed and those who did not would be condemned to Hell.

What Pastor Gayle emphasized was not the judgment aspect of the passage, which Willow found disturbing and contradictory to what Pastor Gayle had previously said about Hell being a choice. The emphasis was on what Jesus clearly wanted people to be doing: helping those in need. "The central message of Jesus was consistently about bringing love to all your relationships. The kind of love Jesus spoke of is not about feelings, it's about behavior. You show your love by how you treat people, not by how you feel about them."

Willow and Pastor Gayle had gotten into the habit of meeting up in the empty sanctuary after Willow grabbed some snacks and pastor Gayle had finished her post-service duties. This weekly check-in with Pastor Gayle was important to Willow, and the pastor was always willing to speak with her. Willow had previously told her about Mr. Retsof having divine gifts. She did not, however, talk about her nighttime outing in the cemetery. Instead, she wanted to know something about the sermon.

"Pastor Gayle, those verses in Matthew made it sound like bad people would be sent to Hell, but you said Hell was a choice. I don't get it."

The pastor sighed and explained, "Yes, there are many misunderstandings based on what the Bible says. It is our starting point for understanding God, but not our ending point. After all, it was written by people who were as imperfect and flawed as any of us, and to think otherwise is pure folly. Some people feel better about life's unfairness if they can just believe the wicked will ultimately receive eternal punishment, and so these concepts found their way into the scriptures. But if we believe in Christ's central message of love, then we can make better sense of these things. A God of love isn't going to send anyone to Hell, but God also gave us free will. God wants us to *choose* love and light. Many do, and some don't. Do you understand?"

"I think so," Willow replied slowly. "But I sure wish the Bible were clearer about what's what. I think it would make your job easier."

Pastor Gayle considered Willow's question a moment before replying. "True, but that would make it almost too easy."

Willow didn't know what to make of that, so she switched to something else she'd been thinking about. "Gehenna chose Hell, but what if she wishes she hadn't made that choice?" She was remembering when she first looked deep into Gehenna's being, searching for some sign of light. There was something there, buried under all the anger and hate. Some kind of vast sadness.

Pastor Gayle looked weary as she slowly shook her head. "Your heart is in the right place, Willow, which is lovely. But I'm afraid Gehenna made an ultimate choice, and one not easily undone. She has become a being of violence and hatred interested only in causing death and destruction. She must be stopped."

~~~~~~~~~~

The High Lord spoke loud and clear: "Willow, come kneel before the High Lady." Willow rose from the pew where she sat, quarterstaff in hand, and made her way to the front of the chapel to kneel before the High Lady upon her throne. The High Lord continued, "Is there one here today who speaks for this young squire's worth and good intentions?"

Willow's parents stood up from where they sat and spoke in unison, "We gladly speak for this young squire's worth and good intentions, and we do hereby lend her our aid."

Willow snuck a peek behind her at all her classmates, as well as their parents and siblings gathered in Sumner Knight Chapel, an old stone chapel in the sprawling Woodlawn Cemetery. The Medieval Ceremony is commonly held during the sixth-grade year in many Waldorf schools, coinciding with the completion of making wooden weapons in woodworking class.

Even though everyone knew the High Lady was the art teacher dressed up as a queen from the Middle Ages and the High Lord was Mr. Retsof looking very much like a medieval minstrel in his costume and holding his guitar, it still felt magical. Willow loved how her classmates seemed to be into it as well. Even Tyler refrained from rolling his eyes and didn't utter one snarky comment the whole time. Her classmates had oo-ed and aw-ed over the pale-green fluorite crystal that now topped her staff, and Mr. Retsof had given her a wide smile and nod of approval for successfully completing her quest.

Always being last did have its advantages. After having heard all the rest of her classmates go through their knighting, she now had the words of the oath memorized. When the High Lady said, "Please repeat the oath after me," Willow began speaking the oath before the High Lady could prompt her with the words.

"I will speak the truth and maintain the right. I will protect the poor, the distressed, and all people. I will practice courtesy and kindness to all. I will deplore the allurement of ease and safety. I will maintain honor and the cause of God in every perilous adventure."

The High Lady smiled warmly at Willow. "Then rise and face those gathered here today. Witness now this brave knight.

She is Willow. Willow is strong. Willow is flexible. Willow is compassionate. Willow is wise. Now go forth, Willow, and serve God as you are meant to do."

When Willow returned to her place among her classmates, the High Lady rose from her throne and addressed everyone. "The world needs men and women who cannot be bought; whose word is their bond; who put character above wealth; who will make no compromise with wrong; whose ambitions are not confined to their own selfish desires; who are true to their friends through good and bad; who are not ashamed or afraid to stand for the truth.

"Knights live by a code of chivalry: A knight is sworn to valor. Their heart knows only virtue. Their blade defends the helpless. Their might upholds the weak. Their word speaks only truth. Their wrath undoes the wicked! It is my pleasure to present to you this day these young knights, brave and true."

The parents stood and applauded their children. Then Mr. Retsof began playing a lively medieval melody on his guitar and everyone filed out of the chapel into the cool evening as the sun sank ever closer to the horizon and dusk fell over the cemetery. It had been a warm enough day that most of the class were dressed informally in shorts and t-shirts, but now it was a bit chilly.

Everyone was milling around outside the chapel, taking family pictures and talking. The boys, of course, soon started horsing around with their swords in mock battles with each other. Out of nowhere, Tyler ran past Willow and snatched her quarterstaff from her, disappearing around the back side of the chapel. Willow considered giving chase but decided not to give him the satisfaction. There really wasn't anywhere for him to go as the chapel was at the edge of dense woods that sloped down and away along a hillside. He'd eventually have to come back around to the front of the chapel.

A scream from behind the chapel brought an abrupt halt to all conversation and horseplay. A familiar dread formed in the pit of Willow's stomach. Tyler came back around to the front side of the chapel. He was pale, wincing in pain, and limping severely. His sword was tucked into the belt of his shorts, and he leaned heavily on Willow's staff. She ran over to him and wedged her shoulder under his other arm to help him over to the steps of the chapel to sit down. "What happened back there?" Willow asked, breathless.

Tyler trembled as he talked. "Something *bit* me from behind. Right before it happened, I heard a kind of low growling sound like a dog would make, but I never even saw it. It was pretty dark back there."

Everyone was crowding around Tyler now. He showed the back of his right calf, which was covered in blood and gashed up worse than anything Willow had ever seen in her life. Tyler's parents sprang into action. His father was wearing a plaid, short-sleeved, button-down shirt open over a t-shirt. He quickly took off the plaid shirt and tied it tightly around Tyler's wounded leg to stop the bleeding while his mother ran to get their car and pull it up in front of the chapel. Tyler's father helped him into the back seat, and they sped off to the hospital. Willow knew the word everyone was probably thinking, though no one dared to speak it aloud: *rabies*. The word in Willow's mind, however, was *hellhound*.

~~~~~~~~~~

Before falling asleep that night, Willow read some more in Annabel Harper's journal. Things had been going well with Annabel teaching music at Lincoln Street School, until the journal entry dated Friday, September 17, 1886. Annabel wrote that one of the sixth-grade students, a girl named Elizabeth, was absent that day because of *hysteria*. Willow remembered reading about "hysteria" during the fall Main Lesson block about the Industrial Revolution. It served as a catch-all diagnosis for any behaviors women or girls exhibited that went against the norms of polite society, which covered a lot of ground back in those days.

Annabel wrote, "I am, of course, most concerned about Elizabeth's health, and yet I also wonder if perhaps her 'illness' isn't anything more than the excited imagination of a child. After all, what could be more natural? Society, however, wants to suppress all such fanciful preoccupations as quickly as possible in children. It is not seen as productive or befitting the turning of girls into young ladies or boys into young men."

Willow was impressed by Annabel's forward-thinking attitude and how it ran counter to what was accepted in those days. What she didn't expect was the entry for Monday, September 20, 1886:

"The moment I entered the school, I sensed something was amiss. As I walked along the main hallway toward my classroom, some teachers stared at me. Normal conversations turned to hushed whispers and nervous glances in my direction. In my classroom, there was a note on my desk from the headmaster, Dr. Percy Dexter, on his personal stationery: *Report to my office immediately.*"

Even reading this entry made Willow feel nervous, as if she were somehow in trouble herself.

"I stood in the open doorway of Dr. Dexter's office where he was absorbed in some writing task. I cleared my throat to get his attention. His expression when he looked up at me was grave. He quietly asked me to come in and also to close the door. I did so, and approached his desk, where there were two chairs. He did not invite me to sit down, so I remained standing. What follows may not be his exact words, although I feel as if they are seared into my memory:

"'Two more sixth-grade girls, and even one boy, are being kept at home from school today because of bouts of *hysteria*. These children are continuously humming or singing a song they learned in your music class. Did you teach them a song about faeries last week?'

"I began to explain, saying, 'Yes, I did, but it's just a harmless Gaelic lullaby—'

"The headmaster cut me off. 'Silence! I am not interested in your explanations. Recite the lyrics of this song you taught them.' Dutifully, I spoke the words of the song about faeries in the moonlight calling children out to spirit them away to their mysterious faery mound.

"When I finished, the headmaster's anger seemed to increase. 'The children also claim they are *seeing* faeries. Are you not aware of the superstitions that still exist about faeries snatching children away from their homes? Do you have any understanding of how you've stained the reputation of this school? None of those children will be coming back. Who knows how many more parents will remove their children from our care. Mrs. Harper, you will go to your classroom, gather your things, and immediately leave the premises. You are no longer welcome in this school.'

"I was too shocked and dismayed to say anything. I stood motionless for a moment while he turned his attention back to the task he had been working on. I wanted to say something in my defense, but it seemed hopeless. I turned and left. I gathered a few things from my classroom and walked out of the school, never to return. I was utterly despondent."

There was more of the journal to read but Willow was very sleepy by this time even while her mind raced about what was happening to Annabel Harper. *Could it be she was an Awakener like Mr. Retsof but somehow didn't know it? Is that even possible? Did she accidentally awaken the Gift of Sight in some of her students and they really were seeing faeries?*

12

MAY DAY ATTACK

---

*"The world's favorite season is the spring.
All things seem possible in May."*

~ EDWIN WAY TEALE ~

The May Day celebration was a beloved ritual at Elm City Waldorf, at least when the weather cooperated. There had been many years where it was cold and rainy, which put a damper on the festivities. This year offered up a warm, sunny day on Sunday, May 1. A crowd of parents and siblings and all the classes from first through eighth grade gathered at the outdoor amphitheater of Robin Hood Park for the event. Families lounged on blankets and younger children played and laughed together. Willow's parents shared a blanket as well. She couldn't imagine a more picture-perfect day than this.

The seventh and eighth grade classes were providing most of the music for the day, playing recorders and string instruments. Mr. Retsof had his trusty guitar. A combined seventh and eighth grade chorus kicked things off with a lovely song loosely based on an old British nursery rhyme reworked to fit a May Day celebration. It was about the cuckoo bird singing his song in the month of May.

They sang it twice through and then started it in a four-part round while Mr. Retsof indicated different sections of the audience to join in on each new part of the round. The air was soon filled with the happy sounds of many voices singing a cheery song that echoed far beyond the amphitheater.

The May Day pole stood tall in the center of the amphitheater's natural "stage" area, festooned with many long, brightly-colored ribbons attached to the top and cascading down in a rainbow of colors. Each class from grades one through five performed a May Pole dance in which the dancers hung onto one or two of the ribbons as they walked or skipped around the pole, moving around each other in a way that weaved the ribbons into a surprisingly intricate pattern, seen and appreciated by all only briefly before the dance reversed and the pattern was unwoven.

Willow loved watching the dances and hearing the music and seeing the sheer joy on everyone's faces. They brought back many memories of the May Day celebrations in which she had taken part, including the four years she had spent at the nursery and kindergarten prior to grade school. Before long, it was time for the sixth-grade sword dance, which would be followed by Willow's solo quarterstaff demonstration. Her heart was beginning to pound in her chest. It was nerve-racking to think she would soon be showing off her moves in front of so many people. She had trained hard during the past four weeks, but there was still so much she had to learn. She knew enough to put on a good show. Or at least she hoped she did.

As for the sword dance, Mr. Retsof had organized the fifteen sword students into three groups of five each. Five dancers were required to form the five-pointed star by interlocking five swords. As the students marched in a circle in time to the music, Mr. Retsof would shout out a move to make with their swords, such as pointing it straight up in the air, bringing them all together to touch tips in the center, and so on. The moves seemed simple enough but performing them while stepping in time to the music was more difficult than it looked.

When the interlocking five-sword star made its first appearance, raised triumphantly over the head of the designated student in each group, the audience gasped in unison at the impressive sight, breaking into spontaneous applause. The star was held high for a turn or two around the circle before Mr. Retsof gave the command for the next sequence. The star was brought back down for the other four students to lay hands on it and precisely break the "lock," as it was called, to disassemble the star and continue another round of the dance. A sense of pride swelled in Willow's breast as she watched her classmates flawlessly execute their sword-dance moves.

And then it was time for Willow to demonstrate the quarterstaff. Dr. Sosserie was nearby, and though no one heard her speak any directions for what Willow was to do, Willow heard her voice clearly in her head. Mr. Retsof began picking out a gentle tune, and Willow was not at all surprised it was that same version of "Coventry Carol" she knew as "When Willows Weep." Willow began to run through all the basic moves she'd learned during her training. These were executed with the grace and precision only a ballet dancer could bring to the task. She was feeling good about her demonstration when a chilly wind began to blow. Thick, dark clouds appeared out of nowhere and blotted out the sun. Everything turned dull and gray.

As she was striking a rather dramatic fighting pose with her staff, the now all-too-familiar feeling of dread made itself known deep in the pit of her stomach. On the far side of the amphitheater where the woods ascended the 130-acre hillside park, a large hellhound with its jagged-striped coat of scraggly fur glared at her with red eyes. A wave of panic began to rise within her. *Oh no, not here, not now. What am I supposed to do?*

The clear, calm voice of Dr. Sosserie eased into her head. "Do you not have the God-given Gift of Fight?"

But I'm not ready for this yet! I've only been training for a few weeks to give a demonstration of quarterstaff technique, not to fight a real battle!

Dr. Sosserie's voice was firm but gentle. "You know more than you think, Willow, and I'll be right here if you need me. No one watching will be the wiser, for they cannot even see this creature of darkness." Willow would have argued more but the hellhound was now trotting toward her.

She glanced at Mr. Retsof, who gave her a nod of his head and changed the music. Instead of the melancholy tune, he turned the same song to a faster tempo with a driving rhythm. His furious strumming made it more like Spanish guitars accompanying Flamenco dances in videos she had watched for one of her dance classes. It filled her with an energy she hadn't felt before: the energy to fight despite her misgivings.

Standing alone in the center of the amphitheater before the unsuspecting crowd of onlookers, Willow assumed a fighting stance as the hellhound broke into a full run toward her. Remembering her many dreams, she anticipated the devil dog would make a leap to try and lock its jaws around her throat. As the creature left the ground and became airborne, Willow crouched down low enough that the dog would sail right over her, but she had more than that in mind. At the precise moment the monster's jaws would have connected with her throat, she thrust upward with all her might. She felt a crunch as the staff connected squarely under the creature's jaw, sending it into a spiraling trajectory behind her.

Willow whirled around to see the dog hit the ground, flailing and scrabbling to right itself and turn back around to face her. Those red eyes were now ablaze with frenzied anger. Willow knew it would not try the same attack again. *What will it do now?*

The calm voice sounded again in her head: "On guard, Willow. If it doesn't go high, it will probably—"

Go low. Got it. I was thinking the same thing.

"See? You're a natural."

There is absolutely nothing natural about any of this, but I get what you're saying.

Sure enough, the hound began a series of darting attacks down low, lips curled back in an evil snarl, aiming to latch onto one of Willows legs with its double rows of fangs. Willow struck the ground firmly with her staff to block each attempt. Then the devil dog did something she hadn't anticipated; it locked its jaws around the staff itself, and its grip was strong.

Willow tightened her two-handed grip on the upper part of the staff. *At least it can't bite me while it's latched onto my staff.* With her weapon otherwise occupied, she did the only thing she could do. She kicked the dog hard in the belly with her right foot. The creature didn't budge as it tried to wrench the staff from her grip. She kicked again, and yet again. The third kick was enough to dislodge it from the staff. It sprang backward out of reach as Willow swung the staff at it, hoping the fluorite crystal would connect with the creature's head. No such luck.

By now Willow was flushed and sweaty despite the chilly wind continuing to blow. Black clouds swirled in the skies above her head. She was losing steam and wasn't sure how much longer she could keep up the frantic pace of this battle. The monster, on the other hand, seemed unfazed as it considered its next move.

But now it was Willow's turn to do something to catch the dog off guard. Everything she'd done so far was of a defensive nature, reacting to the attacks of the creature. It was time for her to go on the offensive. She charged the hellhound with everything she had left in her, but the devil dog responded by also charging headlong toward her. In her mind's eye, she saw the image of her and Gwump vaulting over the stream on her forest quest. It was the perfect move for this moment.

Mid-charge, she planted the iron-sheathed bottom end of her staff firmly on the ground, but instead of vaulting herself high into the air, she used it as leverage to throw both feet in front of her, thrusting her entire body parallel to the ground, like an arrow shot from a bow. It was too late for the hound to stop its charge. Both of Willow's feet connected squarely with the creature's head, breaking its neck with an audible snap. Somehow Willow managed to land on her feet, staff still firmly in her grasp.

Breathing hard and trembling all over, Willow turned to look at the body of the monster lying still on the ground. After a moment, it disappeared in a puff of black ash carried off by the cold wind. The clouds parted and the sun burst through in a triumphant blaze of springtime glory. Dr. Sosserie strode toward her, "Well done, Willow. Well done." They bowed to each other as was their custom, then Willow turned to face the audience, who were now all on their feet clapping and cheering. She bowed to the audience, then promptly fainted in a heap on the ground.

~~~~~~~~~~

Willow opened her eyes slowly, cradled in her father's arms. He was smiling in a worried kind of way. Mom's face was there too, looking very concerned. Willow sat up slowly. They were on the blanket, still at the May Day celebration. Families were milling around talking and sharing snacks from a potluck buffet they had assembled. She sat quietly, just taking in the calm joy of it all. She was also wondering what in the world she should say to her parents. Dad broke the silence first.

"I know you've been working hard at your training during Movement Class with Dr. Sosserie, but I had no idea how good at this you are. Willow, what you did out there was… incredible. It was stunning. It was fierce and beautiful, graceful and powerful. I'm so proud of you!"

Willow expected Mom to counter Dad's enthusiasm with something less gushy, and she did start off that way: "Willow, you're clearly dehydrated and should be drinking more water when you're doing all this crazy training," but then softened and went on to say, "and you were utterly amazing out there. Who knew all your dancing skills could be used like a martial art? Do you remember the dancing-fighting we used to see when we were in Brazil called capoeira? It reminded me of that."

Willow did remember seeing many demonstrations of that curious martial art when they lived for a year on the Island of Santa Catarina off the southern coast of Brazil. It was a magical year of her life she'd hopefully never forget. Having recovered from her fainting spell, she found she was both hungry and thirsty.

"Thanks, Mom and Dad. I'm glad you liked my demonstration. Now I'm starving, so I'm going to get some snacks and hang out with my friends, okay?" She got up and headed to the buffet table without waiting for an answer.

~~~~~~~~~~

Willow went to bed early that night at her mom's request, who also made her drink a ridiculous amount of water beforehand. She would definitely be getting up in the middle of the night to pee, which she hated. She reached into the recesses of her closet and fished out Annabel Harper's diary. She needed to find out what happened next after she was fired from her teaching job.

The subsequent entries were awful to read, but Willow couldn't put the diary down. In the days after being dismissed from the school, Annabel described being the object of much gossip around town. She could see people passing by in front of her house, pointing and whispering. The local daily newspaper ran a few stories with phrases like "dereliction of duty" and "filling the heads of children with unwholesome ideas." Annabel wished she could just shrug them all off. Perhaps she could have, but her husband couldn't.

As the days passed, Annabel's husband became increasingly silent and grim. She recounted her pleading words with him: "I promise you I did nothing wrong. It was just a simple, sweet lullaby: nothing more." His only response was to furrow his brow even deeper, his mouth a tight-lipped line of silence, and stalk out of the room to some other part of the house. Annabel wrote in despair, "My husband has only contempt for me now. Alas! I cannot make him understand I did nothing intentional. My only consolation is my precious baby Jack. He still loves me unconditionally. He is all that matters now."

Annabel didn't think things could get any worse—until they did. Her husband came home one day and announced, "I was dismissed from the firm today because of *you*."

She couldn't have imagined being the object of such scorn from her own husband. "This news made me feel physically ill. I took to my bed for the rest of the evening, right into the night. My husband did not join me. It was a dark night of restless, fitful sleep. Upon waking the next morning, I knew immediately something was wrong. The house was utterly silent: a thick, foreboding, oppressive silence like none I'd ever before experienced. I sprang from my bed and rushed to the nursery. Baby Jack's crib was empty! Frantically I visited every room of the house to no avail. My husband was gone, and he had taken baby Jack with him. I knew in my heart at that moment I would never see either of them again. I am ruined."

After that, the diary entries became increasingly unhinged and weren't dated at all, but Willow already knew the end date from the gravestone she'd seen that moonlit night in the cemetery. Annabel's handwriting was devolving rapidly. It wasn't clear to Willow how the poor woman was surviving in terms of money or food. She never mentioned leaving the house at all. She would rant for pages on end about how she had been grievously wronged by the school, by the town, by her husband.

Annabel's words and tone turned from shocked to sad to indignant to spiteful to hateful from page to page. The writing became less and less legible. She began writing of being visited by someone she called The Dark One. Willow had a very bad feeling about this person. Annabel dutifully copied down everything The Dark One said to her.

"My poor, dear Annabel. I know all too well what it feels like to be scorned by the world, to have everything taken away from you by those who make false accusations and find fault where there is none. You are blameless, my dear Annabel. Never forget this: you have been deeply wronged. I understand exactly what you are going through, for I too was once in your position. I too was blamed for anything and everything wrong in the world. I may be the *only* one who truly understands your current plight."

Willow couldn't understand why Annabel would so willingly accept The Dark One's whisperings. He affirmed her every rant and encouraged her feelings of ill will toward everyone. Then he began to quietly speak words of revenge to her.

"The people who have wrongly accused you are the ones who should be punished. You, who have done nothing wrong, have been ruined by their wagging tongues, their lies, their gossip, and their need to blame someone, anyone, for what they themselves cannot understand. But *you* could be the one to set things right, Annabel. It is *you* who could punish *them*, all of them, for what they've done to you. Name them, Annabel. Name all those who have made your life miserable."

Annabel had written many names in the diary—pages of names. The parents of the hysterical children. The headmaster who dismissed her from the school. The husband who stole her baby Jack and abandoned her. The townsfolk who pointed and whispered and gossiped.

The Dark One's words were chilling to read: "You can get back at all of them, Annabel. Isn't that what you want? I can help you take your revenge. I am the *only* one who help you do this."

Willow could hardly read the scratching on the page that barely passed for writing. Annabel was so far gone by this time she would do anything The Dark One told her to do. Willow was horrified at what he told her to do in order to end her pain and misery. He made it sound easy. It was what she had to do to start over. The last entry in the journal was the worst one of all to read: *"Tonight I go to The Dark One. Annabel will cease to be."*

Tears were streaming down Willow's cheeks as she closed the diary and put it back in its hiding place. It was too horrible. Annabel Harper had been tricked by The Dark One into making a fatal choice.

13

TYLER'S DARK DESCENT

> *"At times our own light goes out and is rekindled by a spark from another person. Each of us has cause to think with deep gratitude of those who have lighted the flame within us."*
>
> ~ ALBERT SCHWEITZER ~

It had happened gradually, but there was no denying it. Tyler's inner light was fading, and Willow didn't know what to do about it. Not knowing whether the animal that bit him at the Medieval Ceremony had rabies or not, his parents wanted to err on the side of safety and had him treated for the dreadful disease. The treatment wasn't pleasant, either. It involved a series of five shots over the course of two weeks. That would be enough to make anyone cranky. Willow, however, knew the truth. He'd been bitten by a hellhound. She could see he had been infected with darkness, and it was taking a toll on him. He wasn't just being cranky; he was becoming mean. His usual good-natured-if-arrogant smirk had become a permanent scowl. Willow feared the darkness would overtake him entirely, and then he'd be... evil? She shuddered at the thought.

What mystified her, however, was how Mr. Retsof couldn't seem to see it. Tyler's behavior was getting worse and worse during class, requiring ever sterner rebukes from Mr. Retsof and even a couple trips to the office. But when Willow brought it up with him in private, he seemed to brush it off as typical "boy" behavior; it was a phase he'd be better off working through within the boundaries of the class. Willow was far less sure about this approach.

She tried talking to Luke about it one day during lunch break since he was Tyler's best friend.

"What's really going on with Tyler? He just seems so grumpy and out of sorts all the time."

Luke sounded as if he had taken a page right out of Mr. Retsof's playbook: "I know, right? He's a big, fat cranky pants lately, but I think it's just a phase. That dog bite really did a number on him. He won't even let anyone look at his leg. That's why he's been wearing pants all the time when I know he'd rather be wearing shorts."

One afternoon a couple weeks after the May Day celebration, Mr. Retsof took the whole class up into the woods of Robin Hood Park. They played an epic game of capture the flag, made all the more exciting by having their weapons with them, which gave it the feel of a medieval battle. Everyone was spread out through the woods, creeping about and making secret plans for their next move in hushed whispers with fellow teammates. At one point, Willow had become separated from her team and wasn't sure where she was in relation to home base. She didn't mind taking a break, though. She wandered the woods, keeping one ear alert to whether anyone might be nearby. And then she saw something she wished she'd never seen.

She could see Tyler, sword in hand, standing still at the base of a tree and not moving a muscle. Willow couldn't imagine what in the world he was doing until she saw an unsuspecting gray squirrel descending the trunk, just far enough to one side of the tree that it didn't see Tyler. *Surely he isn't going to—*

Before she could even finish the thought, Tyler jabbed his sword forward, crushing the squirrel's head. It fell the rest of the way to the ground, twitching as it died.

Willow stared in disbelief. A shuddering began deep inside her. Something was welling up. She was afraid it might be tears. It was *anger*. Stepping into the clearing around the tree where Tyler had done the awful deed, she confronted him. "*Tyler!*" she yelled. "What in the world is wrong with you? Why would do such a horrible, cruel thing?"

Tyler whirled around to face her with a wild look in his eyes. "It's just a stupid squirrel, Willow. Get over it."

The fact he didn't even do his usual *"Wee-low"* version of her name just confirmed the worst of what Willow was thinking. Tyler was being pulled headlong into a world of darkness.

"But Tyler," she pleaded, "that poor squirrel was just minding its own business. There was no reason to kill it. No reason at all!"

Tyler's scowl deepened. "How do you know? How do you know it doesn't have *rabies*? If it has rabies, then it has to be put down. And I can tell you being bitten by a rabid animal is no fun. It sucks, Willow. Trust me, it sucks big time."

Willow wasn't having any of it. "Oh, so now every animal has rabies? I don't think so, Tyler. It's like you've become warped in the head now or something."

Tyler was working himself into a fit of anger. "You don't know anything about my head, Willow, so back off. You may think you're hot stuff with your fancy stick, but you're not. Just go away and leave me alone. Beat it!"

"I'm not going anywhere until you admit what you did was wrong and apologize for it."

"You're even stupider than I thought if you think I'm going to apologize. To whom? The squirrel is *dead*, Willow, so I don't think it's going to care whether I'm sorry. And I'm *not* sorry. Not one bit."

"Then apologize to *me*, Tyler. Tell me you're sorry for killing that poor, innocent animal," Willow's anger was fading into sympathy for this broken boy in front of her. *It wasn't really his fault, was it? At least, not entirely. He was happy just a few weeks ago.* "Tell me… Tell me what's going on with you, Tyler. I want to help."

"*I don't want your help!* I don't need your help. *Go away* now or…" Tyler was shaking with rage.

Willow was alarmed by his fury. She thought she could maybe calm him down and talk some sense into him, but she could see it wasn't going to happen. "Or what, Tyler? Are you going to attack me with your sword? Go ahead. I'd be happy to show you why the quarterstaff *always* beats the sword."

With a shriek, Tyler rushed at her, swinging his sword with wild abandon: no form, no discipline, no thought, no *training*. Willow spun to one side and smacked him in the back with her staff, but not hard. This only served to increase Tyler's rage. He came at her again. This time she flipped her staff and darted the butt end forward, hitting Tyler in the gut. He fell to his knees, gasping for air.

Willow backed away from him. "Okay, Tyler, that's enough. I don't want to hurt you."

Tyler glared at her, then sprang up and charged at her again. Willow ducked down to one side and used her staff to trip him. He fell flat on his face. She was starting to feel bad about all this, knowing it wasn't even a fair fight.

Tyler wasn't moving. He was sprawled out face down on the ground, completely still. *Wait a minute, what if he's really hurt?* This wasn't what she wanted to happen. She didn't even know where they were in the woods or what direction to run in to get help. She took a few deep breaths to stop the wave of panic threatening to wash over her. Dropping her quarterstaff, she knelt beside Tyler and carefully rolled him over, revealing a very angry-looking lump on his forehead, and the rock he'd been unlucky enough to fall on. He was out cold, or at least she was *hoping* he was just knocked out.

Being unconscious, his scowl was gone. He looked the way Tyler *should* look, as if he was peacefully sleeping after a school day full of good-natured teasing and fun with friends. This was the Tyler she knew and liked. In fact, she liked him a *lot* if she was honest with herself. She leaned in and put her own face very close to his. She could feel breath coming out of his nostrils. He was breathing. Thank goodness he was breathing normally, as far as she could tell. Then it occurred to her to do something while she had the chance. She wanted to see his wounded leg for herself.

Which leg had been bitten by the hellhound? She pictured him coming around from the back of the chapel in the cemetery, heavily favoring his right leg. *Yes, it was his right leg.* She lifted his right leg at the knee so it would bend and stay in that position, then worked his pants leg up high enough to inspect his right calf where the devil dog bit him. What she saw nearly made her gag.

It was putrid. The wound looked even worse than it did the day he was bitten, and that was nearly a month ago. It was black, as if the open wound had been smeared with tar.

He was infected with darkness, and it was beyond grotesque. As she stared at the wound, the black substance began to shift and ripple until it took on the shape of Gehenna's veiled form. Willow shrank back in terror.

She needed to do something to help Tyler, but what? He hadn't done anything to deserve this. If only she'd given chase to him at the chapel, she could have fought off the hellhound before it bit him, though she wondered if she would have had the confidence to do so. It wasn't until the May Day battle she became confident in her ability to use her Gift of Fight. She was at a complete loss for what to do, so she offered up a quick prayer. *I'm open to suggestions here, God.* Instinctively, she reached for her quarterstaff. The moment she laid her hands on it, the fluorite crystal began to glow softly. *What the heck?* Then she realized the light was coming from her. It was her own Light, flowing from within her, down her arms, through her hands, and up her staff to the fluorite crystal, which was now shining brightly.

She wasn't sure why or how this was happening, but she had a strong sense she was to use this light flowing through the fluorite crystal to treat Tyler's infection. She did feel a certain satisfaction in laying the brightly glowing crystal right on top of the form of Gehenna in his blackened wound. There was a hissing, crackling sound but otherwise it didn't seem like anything was happening. With effort, Willow intensified her light even more. The hissing and crackling grew louder and finally the black mass of tar-like substance moved off Tyler's leg, becoming a blob-like shape that sank down into the ground and was gone. His leg was still wounded, but it looked the way you'd expect a nasty dog bite to look nearly four weeks later with healing well underway.

Willow's light stopped flowing just as Tyler's eyes fluttered open. He propped himself up on his elbows, wincing from what Willow could only assume must be one of the worst headaches of his life. Looking at his calf, his eyes grew wide, then he looked at Willow with his head cocked to one side, as if he were trying to sort something out in his mind.

"The infection is gone! I don't know what you did or how you did it, but thanks," he said with a genuine smile. He looked down at the ground and his tone became serious. "And I *am* sorry about that poor squirrel. Killing innocent animals for no reason is not my thing at all. I was doing horrible things and I couldn't stop myself. It was like I was watching myself do these things and I was powerless to stop any of it. It was *awful*."

"Well, it's over now, thank goodness," Willow said. "I'm just sorry you went through all that. I don't even know what I did to make it go away. I'm just glad you're back to your usual self."

Tyler added, "That was a pretty stellar move with the staff, by the way, to trip me up."

A genuine compliment from Tyler? For something athletic done by a girl? This is one for the history books!

They sat for a moment just kind of looking at each other, and then both became embarrassed about looking at each other.

Willow tried to fill the awkward silence: "Gosh, we've been out here a long time. We should probably go find everyone else. But you know if we walk out of these woods *together*..."

Tyler smiled another real smile and said, "I don't care what they think. It'll give them something to gossip about for the rest of the week and then it'll die down. I mean, I don't care if *you* don't care."

Willow's reply came a little too quickly, "No, I don't care. I mean I don't mind if they think, uh, I mean if they wanna gossip about it, go right ahead, right?" *Smooth, Willow, real smooth.*

"Cool. Then let's go." Tyler got up a little slowly to test his steadiness. Willow stood up quickly and immediately fainted, right into Tyler's arms. As she drifted off into blackness, she thought, *Oh great. I save him from being infected by the darkness of Hell but* he *gets to carry* me *out the woods?*

~~~~~~~~~~

Willow awoke just as Tyler emerged from the woods into the amphitheater carrying her in his arms, along with her quarterstaff. The entire class, including Mr. Retsof, stood there gaping at them. Of course, there were raised eyebrows and lots of whispering. But honestly, Willow didn't care as much as she thought she would. Tyler wasn't much bigger than her, but he was definitely a lot stronger. And he smelled…good? It was a curious odor she didn't even know how to describe, but whatever it was, she liked it. She didn't mind him carrying her at all. He set her down as Mr. Retsof quickly strode toward them with a look on his face of equal parts concern and potential anger at Tyler, assuming he'd been up to no good. "What happened? We were about to start searching the woods for you two!"

Tyler looked sheepish as he explained, "I fell and hit my head on a rock," he indicated the rather nasty looking lump on his forehead. "Willow found me and woke me up, but then she fainted and I had to carry her."

Mr. Retsof looked relieved. "Well, I'm glad you're both okay. I was worried. Tyler, it was very chivalrous of you to carry Willow through the woods to get her back here safely.

Well done. The actions of a true knight. Willow, you should be drinking more water. You look dehydrated."

What is it with everyone telling me to drink more water? Like it's the go-to thing to whip out when an adult has no clue what the heck is going on? "Yes, Mr. Retsof, I will."

By the time they all made their way back to the school, it was nearly time for dismissal. Willow shook Mr. Retsof's hand, then grabbed her backpack and her quarterstaff. She didn't feel physically up to training, but she wanted to talk to Dr. Sosserie about what happened today.

As she reached the back door of the school that led to the playground, Tyler caught up with her just long enough to say, "You're pretty good with that stick of yours, you know."

Willow decided to give him a little taste of his own medicine. "Yes, actually, I *do* know," then followed up with, "but thanks, Tyler. I appreciate you being man enough to admit it." He gave her his signature smirk as he got into his dad's car and Willow continued to the upper yard to meet Dr. Sosserie.

The doctor was there, leaning on her walking stick. They bowed to each other. Dr. Sosserie took a good look at Willow and said, "You look like you need to—"

"Drink more water. I know, I know," Willow said with an exasperated sigh.

"I'm supposed to be the Telepath here, child," the doctor said with mock indignation and a chuckle. "But I do sense something significant has occurred to you today."

Willow hurriedly explained everything that happened in the woods with Tyler. Well, all the pertinent facts at any rate. The doctor's raised eyebrow indicated she had a sense she wasn't getting the full story. When Willow was finished, Dr. Sosserie nodded her head in approval.

"It seems you *do* in fact have a third divine gift—the Gift of Light. But you must be very careful with this gift, Willow. There are consequences to using your own light. It will deplete you physically, as you've already experienced from your fainting spell. It also depletes you spiritually. You gave up some of your Light to help another. Admirable, yes, but also dangerous. In your depleted state, you're more vulnerable, though it's a temporary effect. Your Light will 'recharge' soon enough with rest and plenty of fluids, so we won't do any heavy training today."

I can heal people with my Light? That is too cool! "I do get what you're saying about it taking a lot out of me. I definitely feel kind of rundown." *Actually, I feel completely crappy right now.*

14

GEHENNA'S LAST STAND

> *"If you know the enemy and know yourself, you need not fear the result of a hundred battles. If you know yourself but not the enemy, for every victory gained you will also suffer a defeat. If you know neither the enemy nor yourself, you will succumb in every battle."*
>
> ~ SUN TZU ~

The end of the school year was suddenly in sight, which took everyone by surprise. The last day of school was typically planned for mid-June, but then there were always some number of snow days that would end up extending school by at least another week, but not this year. This past winter had been milder than usual, and spring had arrived earlier than anyone could remember. June 6–10 would be the last week of school.

On Monday of that week, Mr. Retsof made an announcement that had the class buzzing with excitement: "We'll celebrate the close of sixth grade with an overnight camping experience at Maple Lane Farm up at the end of Old Gilsum

Hill Road in the apple orchards there. The school owns several large tents we'll set up in the orchard Friday evening at eight. I've given a list to your parents of items you should each have with you. To finish our year on the medieval theme, bring your weapons. It's going to be a full moon, and we'll have some fun sparring by moonlight."

Willow envisioned taking on Tyler and kicking his butt by moonlight. *Not exactly romantic, but...*

When Friday arrived, much of the afternoon was taken up with the eighth-grade graduation ceremony held in the large backyard of Dr. Sosserie's house, which was just down the street from the school. The contribution of the sixth-grade class to the event was the closing song: an a cappella rendition of a pop song they had been working on since May Day. Mr. Retsof arranged his own version of it for them to sing, toning down the pop music flavor and making it more "Waldorfy" as Willow liked to put it. The song was "Unwritten" by Natasha Bedingfield, and the final lines of the refrain about living life with arms wide open and the rest being still unwritten seemed an especially appropriate send-off to whatever would come next for the graduates.

Later that evening, parents brought their sixth graders up to the orchard and said their goodbyes. Willow lived down the road from the orchard and had walked up with her backpack, sleeping bag, and quarterstaff. Mr. Retsof divided the class up into four groups: two groups of boys and two groups of girls. He got them started setting up the four large tents while he set up his own smaller tent. They worked quickly as the sun was already low on the horizon. There were still a surprising number of blossoms on the rows and rows of apple trees, and their fragrance filled the air. The orchard was surrounded by a tall chain-link fence to keep the deer out.

By the time they finished setting up the tents and stowing their backpacks and sleeping bags inside it was fully dark, but the gigantic, full moon was the brightest Willow had ever seen. It bathed the entire orchard in silvery moonlight that made it easy to see everything. Mr. Retsof had lit a small campfire and produced the requisite marshmallows, graham crackers, and chocolate bars for everyone to enjoy a round or two of s'mores, or three in the case of most of the boys as Willow noticed. *Why do boys lack all self-control when it comes to sweets?* Not that girls don't enjoy sweets too, but the way the boys stuffed their faces always struck her as gross.

As they sat around the fire, Mr. Retsof strummed his guitar absentmindedly. Willow looked around at all her classmates who were uncharacteristically silent as they stared into the fire, mesmerized by the dancing flames. It suddenly hit her how much she loved them all, even though each of them had their foibles and annoying traits. She tuned in to their inner Light and all was well. Each had a strong glow, including Tyler. She had found herself checking up on his Light more frequently since the whole hellhound-darkness-infection episode, but he seemed entirely over it, and even a better person because of it. *Nothing like a little case of demonic possession to straighten out a teenage boy and put the fear of God in him, I guess.*

The soft, familiar voice she had heard whisper in her head that "Darkness is coming" was there again, but with a new and startling message. This time the voice said, "Darkness is here." She finally recognized it. It was the voice of the woman who was her preschool teacher at the Elm City Waldorf Nursery and Kindergarten, Ms. Skörbo. *She must be gifted too.*

Before Willow could give it any more thought, a blood-curdling howl tore through the cool night air, startling everyone out of their individual reveries. Her classmates were frozen in place, wide-eyed with fear. Another howl sounded from a different direction, and then another. They sounded distant, but even at a distance was too close for comfort.

In a very shaky voice, Harmonie voiced what was on everyone's minds: "Wh-what was *that*?"

Tyler tried to put on a brave face. "Just a few coyotes, probably." But the number of howls was increasing, overlapping into a cacophony of howls punctuated with furious barking. And it sounded like it was getting closer.

Luke spoke up, "Sounds more like *wolves* than coyotes to me, and a *lot* of them."

Camille looked like she was about to burst into tears as she said, "But the fence will keep them out, right? *Right?*"

All eyes turned to Mr. Retsof, who was now standing and looking a bit pale. "Ah, well, the fence—"

Willow leaped to her feet and interrupted, "Okay, they're not coyotes. But they're not wolves either. They're *hellhounds*. Like the thing that bit Tyler after the Medieval Ceremony. If they find a way to get through the fence—and trust me when I say they will—we'll be in big trouble. We need to get out of here right now!" She wanted to get everyone moving rather than focusing on their fear.

Mr. Retsof sprang into action. "Everyone grab your weapons and leave everything else—*now!*" He turned to Willow, "Make contact with Dr. Sosserie and tell her to get everyone up here as quickly as possible."

"Um, okay," Willow replied. *Who does he mean by "everyone?"* She already had her quarterstaff in her hands, but she really didn't know how to contact the doctor. Dr. Sosserie could speak to her telepathically, but Willow didn't know how to initiate a conversation with her. By now everyone had their swords in hand and were gathered together. Mr. Retsof had his guitar slung across his back.

Tyler seemed like he was itching for a fight. "What's the plan?" He asked. His question was not directed at Mr. Retsof. He asked it to Willow. If she weren't shaking in her shoes, she might have smiled.

"There's a back entrance to the orchard. We'll go out that way, then cut down through the woods and across the hay field to my house. We'll be safer there." She wasn't at all sure if this would be the case, but it sounded good. Tyler nodded his assent.

"Okay, Willow," Mr. Retsof with determination. "Lead the way."

She glanced at her assembled classmates, still wide-eyed with fear. She was pretty sure a couple of them were crying. "Let's go!" She turned and ran down the gentle slope between rows of apple trees to the back gate door in the fence, undid the latch, and threw it open wide. Thank goodness for a bright, full moon so they could see where they were going. As she ran, she thought out a message to the doctor: *Dr. Sosserie? Are you there? Hellhounds are attacking* now, *and we need all the help we can get!*

She was surprised by a near-instantaneous response from the doctor. "We'll be there in a couple minutes. Don't worry."

Willow had no idea how that could happen, seeing as it was at least a ten-minute drive to her house from anywhere downtown.

They were a noisy bunch crashing down through the woods, but it wasn't like they were going to be able to hide from the hellhounds no matter what they did. When they reached the far end of the hay field, there was the broken-down barn and Willow's little yellow house on the other side of it. Her willow tree stood tall and graceful in the moonlight.

As they ran down the gentle slope of the hayfield toward the barn, they could hear the hellhounds getting closer. Their howling was unbearably loud. Then, as they drew nearer to the barn, it exploded into a raging inferno of violent flames. How could that even happen? Now they were trapped, just like in her dream.

Around the side of the barn came a group of four people. It was Dr. Sosserie, Mr. O'Norscon, Pastor Gayle, and a skinny African American boy Willow didn't know. The doctor unsheathed the rapier from her walking stick. Mr. O'Norscon was wielding a Thor-like hammer, and even Pastor Gayle had something. It was the candlelighter from church, which seemed an unlikely weapon. Only the Black boy carried no weapon whatsoever.

Dr. Sosserie answered the question Willow was thinking. "He's how we got here so quickly. He's powerfully gifted, but using his gift to get us here was a huge effort and has left him thoroughly weakened." Willow had no idea what gift he might have, but she nodded at the boy, and he nodded back.

The hellhounds had arrived, pouring into the hayfield from all sides. Dozens turned into hundreds, and hundreds soon became thousands. The field was writhing with them and the howling was beyond deafening. The beasts were no longer hiding behind their veil of invisibility. They *wanted* to be seen. This was not helping the courage of Willow's classmates, who were stricken with fear.

Dr. Sosserie took Willow and Mr. O'Norscon aside. "There are far too many of them and too few of us with the Gift of Fight. This is not a battle we can win without substantial assistance."

"And yet fight we must, no?" Mr. O'Norscon said gruffly. "If we don't try, the consequences will be all the more devastating."

They both turned to Willow. *Why are they looking at me? I don't have any idea what to do.* And then it came to her. It was so simple! "The will-o-wisps! They're beings of pure light, and the hellhounds are beings of pure darkness, right? If we can summon the will-o-wisps, maybe they can help us!"

She pulled Mr. Retsof over and shouted to him above the clamor of devil dogs. "Play whatever song you think might attract the will-o-wisps! Dr. Sosserie, do whatever you can to make contact with any of them telepathically. Pastor Gayle, pray to God to send us as many will-o-wisps as possible."

Willow ran around the side of the burning barn and knelt at the base of her willow tree. She put her staff on the ground and placed both hands on the trunk of the tree. *I know you can communicate with other trees. Please spread the message through your underground network. We need will-o-wisps here as quickly as possible.* She didn't even know if trees and will-o-wisps could communicate with each other, but it seemed worth trying.

Mr. Retsof began to play, but no one could even hear it above the din. Dr. Sosserie looked deep in thought. Pastor Gayle laid down her candlelighter and raised her palms upward toward the heavens, mouthing prayers for divine intervention.

Utter silence descended. The hellhounds stopped their howling and became still. At first Willow thought Mr. Retsof had somehow mesmerized them with his music, which could now be heard clearly. She saw what brought a hushed stillness to the vast horde of devil dogs. Floating toward them from the far end of the field, just above the heads of the hounds, was Gehenna, looking as formidable and terrifying as ever.

The dreadful, screeching voice she had hoped never to hear again ripped its way into her head. She could tell by the way her classmates put their hands over their ears that they heard it too. They didn't realize there was nothing they could do to stop hearing it. "This is the best you could do? This is the army you've assembled to battle mine? A ragtag handful of children with wooden swords? How utterly…*delightful*. My hellhounds will tear you all to shreds." Her cackling laughter was searing pain in everyone's heads.

Willow looked around in desperation. Her classmates were cowering in fear. The adults looked worried. Gehenna seemed larger than life. The horde of hellhounds kept growing larger. Willow began to doubt any of this could go their way. It was as if her recurring nightmare was about to come true. She wasn't feeling "special" at all. She felt utterly powerless. Hope was fading fast. And then a miracle happened.

Will-o-wisps began appearing among the fearful group of fighters. One alighted on the tip of each of her classmates' swords and one on the tip of the doctor's rapier. Several settled on different parts of Mr. Retsof's guitar, and several more landed upon Mr. O'Norscon's hammer. One came to the tip of Pastor Gayle's candlelighter. Three came to light on the fluorite crystal of Willow's quarterstaff. There were dozens more, and they settled throughout the drooping fronds of the weeping willow tree.

Willow turned to the skinny Black kid and said, "You should go hide behind the willow tree. The will-o-wisps will protect you there." The boy seemed relieved and shakily made his way over to the tree and took shelter behind it.

Now everyone turned to Willow. Tyler spoke up: "What do we do now?"

Willow spoke clearly and confidently, praying what she was about to say would be true. "The will-o-wisps are beings of pure light, and the hellhounds are created from pure darkness.

One touch from your weapon with the will-o-wisp on it and a hellhound will be instantly vaporized. So, what we do now is…*we fight!*"

Willow, Dr. Sosserie, and Mr. O'Norscon stood in front to take the brunt of the onslaught to come while Mr. Retsof and Pastor Gayle hung slightly further back with the rest of the class to deal with any hellhounds that might manage to get around to them.

With a swooping gesture of her arms, Gehenna's horde of hellhounds sprang forward to attack. The ensuing melee was a chaos of whirling weapons and snapping jaws. As she had hoped and prayed, each time their weapons struck a hellhound, it burst into a puff of black ash carried away by the nighttime breeze.

On one of her spinning moves, Willow caught a glimpse of something unexpected. There were so many hellhounds it was inevitable some would get around the fighters to go after the Black boy hiding behind the trunk of her willow tree. But her beloved tree was alive in a way she'd never seen. With its drooping branches full of will-o-wisps, the tree was whipping its branches about, taking out hellhounds right and left. The boy was safer under the protection of the tree than anywhere else.

Dr. Sosserie's voice sounded in her head: "Willow, we can't keep this up forever. Gehenna appears to have an endless supply of hellhounds at her disposal. We adults need to protect your classmates above all else. You must stop Gehenna."

Willow was about to protest when the comforting voice of Ms. Skörbo came to her again. "I am a Discerner. The day you first arrived at the preschool, I discerned you had powerful divine gifts within you. I had the clearest vision I've ever had, and it was a vision of you defeating Gehenna."

Is this why everyone thinks I'm special? Because my preschool teacher had a vision about me when I was three years old? But what do they think I'm going to actually do?

Dr. Sosserie's voice in her head was firm: "*Kill* her, Willow. If you don't, she'll continue to wreak havoc wherever she goes. She must be stopped once and for all."

Willow was shocked at what the doctor expected her to do. *I will not kill her. I will stop her. I don't know how, but I will stop her.*

With determination, Willow fought her way through the horde toward Gehenna, clearing the way by whirling her staff every which way. It was a blur of streaking light vaporing hellhounds all around her. Gehenna's voice pierced her brain. "Yes, foolish child, come to me. I've been waiting patiently for this encounter since we last met in the cemetery. Tonight, you will learn a painful lesson about the true power of darkness over this world."

With her attention focused entirely on Willow, the constant flow of new hellhounds ceased. Maybe this would give a chance for the others to finish off the remaining devil dogs and catch their breath. Alone now in the center of the field, the two of them faced off. Willow was aching all over, gasping to catch her breath. Another three will-o-wisps crowded onto the fluorite crystal, and a dozen settled in various positions along the length of the staff. Her weapon was ablaze with the pure, white light.

Gehenna threw her arms forward and pure darkness shot out of them, a thick, black stream hurtling toward Willow. She pointed her staff at it and the will-o-wisps formed a shield of light at its tip. The darkness hit the shield hard, nearly knocking Willow off her feet, but she managed to stay upright. The shield held. Gehenna increased the forceful flow of darkness and Willow began to stumble backward. Another group of will-o-wisps added themselves to the shield. Pushing hard, Willow began to make slow, agonizing progress toward Gehenna. As the demon summoned even stronger darkness, more will-o-wisps joined the shield and Willow pressed on. With one last mighty heave forward, the giant shining shield struck Gehenna in an explosion of light that scattered the will-o-wisps near and far. Gehenna fell backward to the ground and lay still.

The force of the explosion had ripped away Gehenna's veil. Willow was almost afraid to look upon the face of the creature that lay before her, but finally she approached and looked down. Her heart immediately leapt into her throat. The face she saw was one of striking beauty she knew well: the face of Annabel Harper. All the horrible events she had read about in Annabel's journal came flooding back to her. The empathy she felt for what Annabel had gone through, how Annabel hadn't a clue as to why any of it was happening, and the ultimate choice she made in desperation with the promise of exacting revenge against all who had wronged her. Willow understood why she had done the unspeakable. She understood how she became Gehenna, plotting and planning as she grew her powers of darkness in Hell. All this to one day return to Keene to destroy the fae folk, the school, and anyone who stood in her way.

Willow knelt down and placed the back of her hand near Annabel's nose and mouth. Nothing. She was not breathing. Feeling the same panic she felt when Tyler was knocked out in the woods, she grabbed one of Annabel's hands and tried to find a pulse on her wrist, then her neck. Nothing. Gehenna was dead, and so was Annabel Harper for a second time. *No! This is not what I meant to do. I just wanted to stop her!* Willow remembered how she healed Tyler's wound with her own inner Light. Could she bring Annabel back? She grabbed her staff and tried to summon her Light. She wanted to feel it flowing through her arms and hands and into her staff. There was nothing. She was too weak from the fight.

Willow wept. She wept for the tortured soul of Anabel Harper. She wept for all Gehenna's victims. She wept for what she herself had just done. Annabel Harper didn't deserve any of this. No one deserved anything like this. She should have been reunited with her husband and child in Heaven. Annabel Harper deserved redemption as much as anyone else. Willow wept bitter tears for having taken that chance away from her. She didn't mean to kill her. She meant to stop her and convince her God would forgive her if she but pleaded in earnest to be forgiven. But now it was too late. As Willow's tears fell upon Annabel Harper, the body slowly dissolved and faded into the ground. She was gone.

Willow felt hands gently lift her up. It was Pastor Gayle. Willow couldn't stop sobbing. Pastor Gayle enfolded her in a loving embrace, whispering prayers of consolation and asking God to forgive them all for what had happened here tonight and to bring healing to Willow.

Willow was extremely weak now. She could feel herself slipping into unconsciousness. Mr. O'Norscon swept her up into his burly arms. She glanced around wearily, surrounded by her classmates and the mysterious Black boy she didn't know. The will-o-wisps were gone. Her willow tree stood still in the moonlight, looking as it always did. And the broken-down barn looked as it always did. She couldn't understand why it wasn't a pile of ash. Nothing was making any sense, but she didn't care. *What is that look on Tyler's face? Shock? Admiration? Something else?* She let herself drift off into wherever her unconscious mind wanted to take her. Luckily for her, it was into a deep and restful sleep.

15

THE DAY AFTER

"To live in the light of a new day and an unimaginable and unpredictable future, you must become fully present to a deeper truth; not a truth from your head, but a truth from your heart; not a truth from your ego, but a truth from the highest source."

~ DEBBIE FORD ~

Willow wiggled her way out of her sleeping bag as quietly as possible to avoid waking anyone up. Satisfied that Camille, Harmonie, and Lila were still sound asleep, she slipped out of the tent and made a beeline to Mr. Retsof, who was making sure the campfire from yesterday was completely out. The events of last night felt more like remembering a dream than reality, but she knew it had all happened. Mr. Retsof was crouched down, poking around in the fire's remains to see if there were any hot coals left and scraping dirt over it. Willow just stood there watching, trying to figure out where to start. She had so many questions.

At last, her teacher paused and looked up at her. "I know last night was…difficult for you, Willow. But I want you to know you displayed leadership and courage beyond what anyone could reasonably expect of you. And because of your bravery and your determination, all your classmates are safe. The fae folk are safe. Our school and our community are safe. Those are the truths of what took place last night, and they are true because of *you*, Willow."

Yeah, but the truth also includes me having killed someone, and I didn't even mean to do it. That doesn't seem fair. What happened to Annabel Harper wasn't fair. Where is Annabel Harper's soul now? Willow didn't feel like she could speak any of this out loud. She didn't want Mr. Retsof to think she was ungrateful for the positive outcomes he'd just mentioned.

Willow looked back to the four large tents where her classmates dreamed of… What? "How are they going to make sense of everything they saw last night?" This was her biggest concern. She was thinking of Annabel Harper and what can happen to someone who is thrust into a whole new aspect of reality without any understanding of what was happening.

"Fear not, Willow. Your classmates will not remember the events of last night. I sang a very special song to put them to sleep. One that would also make them forget everything about last night's events. They will remember the s'mores, which did happen, and they will remember sparring in the moonlight, which did not happen." A grin spread across his face as he said, "And Tyler will remember beating everyone except for you and your *stick*, of course."

Note to self: Adults are more clued in to what's happening with kids than they let on. "Oh, well, thanks for that, I guess. But what I'm really confused about is the barn. It was totally on fire but then looked like it hadn't been burned at all?"

"Yes, that was rather curious. We think it was an illusion Gehenna created to convince us we were trapped."

Willow didn't see how that was possible. "But you could feel the heat of the flames; it was searing hot to be anywhere near it!"

Mr. Retsof nodded his head in agreement. "Indeed it was. But the most powerful illusions *are* real if you *believe* they are real. When Gehenna was struck down, the flames disappeared and nothing had burned."

"And who was that African American boy?" Willow asked.

"His name is Micah. He's new to the area and will be joining our seventh-grade class in the fall."

Micah was one curious character, and one Willow was looking forward to getting to know better.

Willow's classmates were stirring and beginning to wake up. She watched them emerge from their tents, blinking and squinting in the bright morning sun, stretching, yawning, and rubbing the sleep from their eyes.

These were her people. She loved them all so much. She protected them last night from the powers of Hell itself. She felt good about that, and proud of the praise Mr. Retsof had given her. She didn't think of herself as a leader, let alone a courageous one, and yet that's exactly what she was last night. But at what cost? Try as she might, she could not get the image of a beautiful but dead Annabel Harper out of her head.

Tyler walked over to her and said, "I think I'm still in shock about last night."

Willow was startled out of her thoughts. *Does Tyler remember what really happened last night? Maybe Mr. Retsof's memory-wiping song didn't work on him.* "Uh, yeah, it was pretty crazy, right?"

"Yes, it was," Tyler replied with a smile. "I thought for sure I'd be able to beat you."

Whew! He's talking about the games last night that didn't even happen. "Well, you know, I have been training pretty hard at this for a while now."

"It shows," he said with admiration, then added, "I guess if there's a girl who is going to beat me at anything, I'd want it to be you."

Willow didn't know what to say to that, though she could feel her cheeks getting hot. A long silence made them both feel more than a little awkward.

Parents began to appear outside the orchard's fence in their cars to pick up their kids. This was it. A few of her classmates lived in Keene, but most lived in surrounding towns, including Tyler. She often didn't see many of them again until the next school year because of family vacations and so on.

"I see my parents are here, so I guess I better go," Tyler said. He started to walk away but stopped and turned back to Willow, "If you're, you know, around this summer, maybe we could like, I don't know, hang out or—?"

Willow didn't even let him finish. "Yes!" *Was that too eager? That was too eager.* "I mean, uh, sure. I'd like that." *I'd like that a whole lot.*

Tyler grinned and said, "Cool. I'll give you a call and we'll figure it out. See you later."

Willow smiled the whole walk home. *I think this summer is going to be the best one ever.*

~ THE END ~

ACKNOWLEDGMENTS

Writing a first novel is a daunting undertaking, one made even more difficult in my case because of how I make my living. I am a non-fiction freelance writer and editor for hire. Fiction requires a very different kind of writing from my bread-and-butter non-fiction writing, and yet I decided to tackle a novel for my first book despite knowing this ahead of time. To provide myself with sufficient structure, support, and accountability, I joined the Creator Institute book writing program. The challenge I faced as a non-fiction writer attempting a novel was further confirmed when I started looking at some of the tools the program provides to fiction writers. To me, they appeared to be written in an alien language. I could have easily fled screaming at that point. Instead, I took a deep breath and chose to forge ahead.

The primary acknowledgment for completing this book journey must first and foremost be attributed to my daughter, Willow. Without her, there would be no reason for writing this book. She was my constant confidant and sounding board for what would go into this story. (She is herself the protagonist, after all). Her input and opinions were invaluable. She is a treasure, and without her my life would have infinitely less meaning.

If I have succeeded in what I set out to do, it is due in no small part to the excellent Creator Institute editors I worked with along the way. Some early vital feedback on my first chapter from Senior Developmental Editor Michael Bailey helped me understand how to achieve the desired point of view I was aiming for in the novel, as well as how to do more "showing" than "telling" (my non-fiction writing is almost all telling with very little showing involved). My Developmental Editor, Avery Lockland, provided balanced feedback I found encouraging and very practical in terms of when to avoid or embrace particular tropes of which I would have been otherwise unaware.

Transitioning from the first-draft writing phase with Creator Institute to the publishing phase with New Degree Press introduced a whole new group of people to work with. Natalie Bailey, Video Production Coordinator, and Jennifer Clogg, Video Production Assistant shepherded me through the process of creating a book trailer video to be used for marketing and fundraising (a crowd-funding campaign to cover book production costs). My Acquiring Editor, Blake Hoena, and Head of AE, Venus Bradley, kept after to me to finish the last few chapters of my first draft manuscript during an incredibly busy time when it seemed all my writing clients needed tons of work from me at the same time. Blake's feedback helped me understand where I needed to inject more conflict and move the plot forward.

My Marketing and Revisions Editor, Sarah Lobrot, not only guided me through the fundraising campaign process, but also provided feedback during two full rounds of revisions to my manuscript. Whoever said, "A good novel isn't written, it's rewritten," was definitely not joking! The process was both grueling and rewarding. My novel is much better for it. An additional layer of oversight and encouragement was provided by MRE Wrangler, Kristy Carter, who seems to always know just what to say and when to say it to keep writers moving forward.

I would be remiss if I didn't mention the masterminds behind this grand project of helping first-time authors write and publish their first book as if they're a second-time author: Professor Eric Koester of Georgetown University, who founded Creator Institute, and Brian Bies, Head of Publishing at New Degree Press. Together they have figured out how to make writing and publishing a quality book work for many people who otherwise might not ever make it to the finish line. The hybrid publishing model they've put together gives first-time authors a real shot at getting their book out to the world without signing their lives away in a contract that leaves them little to no control over their book or profits from sales. They have my deepest appreciation for introducing me to a publishing path for first-time authors that makes much more sense than other options.

When it was time to assemble a short video about my book for the pre-sales campaign, I wanted to include some video footage of Keene, New Hampshire, where the story is set. I stumbled across a fellow by the name of Tony Morrison (no relation) who was launching his own drone video and photography business. Sure enough, he had some aerial footage of downtown Keene perfect for what I envisioned, and he was very gracious in making some of his clips available to me, though they didn't end up in the final version of my book video. You can see his work at http://morrisondrone.com or on Facebook at https://www.facebook.com/morrisondrone.

If you'd like to learn more about Waldorf education, a good starting point is the website of the Association of Waldorf Schools of North America (AWSNA) at www.

waldorfeducation.org. If you'd like to take a deeper dive into Waldorf founder Rudolf Steiner's contributions across a stunning array of subject areas, explore the Rudolf Steiner Archive and eLibrary at www.rsarchive.org.

I also want to recognize all the wonderful people who joined my author community through my pre-launch campaign. My deepest thanks to the following individuals who were willing to join and support me on my publishing journey, not only financially, but some also served as beta readers to provide feedback during the manuscript revision process:

Christine King	Jordan Waterwash
ChandaElaine Spurlock	AJ Flanagan
Susan Gettum	Brian Saxby
Tracy McVetty	Donnie Webber
Patricia Giramma	Scott Aronowitz
Judy Rosen	Bruce Elliot
Carl Allen	Shanna Heath
Jean Prior	Barbara Andrews
Elisa Delucia	Andrew Hetes
Eric Koester	Kelly Espenshade
Dan Patterson	Eric Fox
Cass Lauer	Harral Hamilton
George Russell	Kyle Trombley
Carrie Ely	Andrea Farnsworth
Carlo Mahfouz	Don Hackler

Jeffrey Stoutenburgh
Marty Hennum
Melissa Neff
Barb Leatherman
Rose Kundanis
Mark Harris
Martha Ladam
Cynthia Bagley
Pam Doyle
Ella Rank
Marlene Baldwin
Beverly Caldon
Debra Bokum
Marion B. Eckhard
Drew Rowles
Bruce Holloway
Charlotte Traas
Jim Morrison
Sam Ettaro
Lynn Kraihanzel
Joseph Morrison
Marilyn Tullgren
Kathy Blair

Van Weigel
Catherine Behrens
Jim and Jean Bombicino
Veda Crewe
Kathy Halverson
Betty Christiansen
Howeina Lariviere
Damien Licata
Carlee Ranalli
Dianne Patenaude
Sandra Peace-Carey
Rebecca Barrett
Kristen Leach
Julie White
Bridget McBride
Holly Tepe
James Vander Hooven
James (Bill) Hickock
Ryan Sproul
John and Samantha Savage
Lynn and Art Simington
Lucy and Sam Bradley

MY JOURNEY INTO FANTASY

During the summer after sixth grade in 1980, I was sent down to the public middle school I attended one day and had to take a battery of tests. I was only vaguely aware at the time they were IQ tests. When I started the seventh grade, I was placed in the school's "gifted" program. I remember absolutely nothing about the content of the curriculum or programming except for one standout feature: Ms Timko introduced us to a fantasy role-playing game called Dungeons and Dragons. It's entirely possible that playing "D&D" is all we did in that middle school gifted program, and that was fine with me. I was immediately hooked. Creating a character, going on quests, fighting monsters, collecting treasure and artifacts, advancing in levels: I loved it all, and I always created and played magic-user characters. I played D&D avidly for a solid seven years, primarily with a small group composed of my closest friends spanning three grade levels.

When I think about why Ms. Timko would have taken a handful of arguably the most intelligent kids in a public school and allowed them to spend an entire class period playing D&D regularly—something most of our parents probably would have objected to had they been paying closer attention—it's easy to understand the educational value in hindsight. Decision-making, group collaboration, critical thinking: these were all quickly developed and exercised in order to survive and thrive in each fantasy campaign setting. This was not my first exposure to fantasy. I collected comic books (only one title, *The Avengers*, Marvel Comics). I saw the 1977 animated version of *The Hobbit* that aired on NBC. I also saw the 1979 animated version of *The Lion, the Witch and the Wardrobe* that aired on CBS. I saw *Star Wars* in a movie theatre in 1977. But what playing D&D in that middle school gifted program did was make me want to *read* fantasy novels.

This was all happening as I entered adolescence in a small, out-of-the-way town of rural western Pennsylvania back in the early 1980s. The fantasy novels I recall reading for pleasure in those days included J.R.R. Tolkien's *The Hobbit* (but not the *Lord of the Rings* trilogy, for some odd reason), all of Anne McCaffrey's books in the *Dragonriders of Pern* series (the original trilogy and the Harper Hall trilogy), and *The Chronicles of Narnia* by C.S. Lewis. I loved the adventure, the fantasy elements, and the constant struggle between good and evil, often (but not always) so clearly defined. When I think about fantasy as a literary genre, three quotes strike me as especially relevant:

> "Fantasy is a necessary ingredient in living. It's a way of looking at life through the wrong end of a telescope, and that's what makes you laugh at the terrible realities." (Minear, 2001)

> "I have claimed that Escape is one of the main functions of fairy stories, and since I do not disapprove of them, it is plain that I do not accept the tone of scorn or pity with which 'Escape' is now so often used: a tone for which the uses of the word outside literary criticism give no warrant at all...Why should a man be scorned if, finding himself in prison, he tries to get out and go home? Or if, when he cannot do so, he thinks and talks about other topics than jailers and prison walls? The world outside has not become less real because the prisoner cannot see it. In using escape in this way, the critics have chosen the

wrong word, and what is more, they are confusing, not always by sincere error, the Escape of the Prisoner with the Flight of the Deserter." (Tolkien, 1997)

"Fairy tales, then, are not responsible for producing in children fear, or any of the shapes of fear; fairy tales do not give the child the idea of the evil or the ugly; that is in the child already, because it is in the world already. Fairy tales do not give the child his first idea of bogey. What fairy tales give the child is his first clear idea of the possible defeat of bogey. The baby has known the dragon intimately ever since he had an imagination. What the fairy tale provides for him is a St. George to kill the dragon. Exactly what the fairy tale does is this: it accustoms him for a series of clear pictures to the idea that these limitless terrors had a limit, that these shapeless enemies have enemies in the knights of God, that there is something in the universe more mystical than darkness and stronger than strong fear." (Chesterton, 1909)

A lot is happening in that paragraph, but author Neil Gaiman paraphrased it nicely when he wrote, "Fairy tales are more than true: not because they tell us dragons exist, but because they tell us dragons can be beaten." (Gaiman, 2002) Gaiman wanted to use some or all of the Chesterton passage as an epigraph in his novel, so he jotted down his own paraphrase of it and mistakenly attributed his paraphrased version of the quote to Chesterton.

I share these thoughts about fantasy and my own path into this genre as a way of encouraging everyone to explore it more fully. There are so many variations in styles of fantasy that there is surely something for everyone. Enjoy your own journey!

BIBLIOGRAPHY

A NOTE FROM THE AUTHOR
Lloyd Alexander Documentary. "A Visit with Lloyd Alexander." January 30, 2018. 21:39. https://youtu.be/Wt9ZHQy2wAk

ACKNOWLEDGMENTS
Chesterton, G.K. *Tremendous Trifles*. New York: Dodd, Mead and Company, 1909, pp. 129-130.

Gaiman, Neil. *Coraline*. New York: HarperCollins, 2002, epigraph in the front matter pages of the original edition.

Minear, Richard H. *Dr. Seuss Goes to War: The World War II Editorial Cartoons of Theodor Seuss Geisel*. New York: The New Press, 2001, pp. 260-261.

Tolkien, J.R.R. *The Monsters and the Critics And Other Essays*. London, UK: George Allen & Unwin, 1983, pp. 147-148.

www.ingramcontent.com/pod-product-compliance
Lightning Source LLC
LaVergne TN
LVHW011832060526
838200LV00053B/3991